Scotland's Knight:
The Rose in the Glade

by

Anne K. Hawkinson

Paul V. Hunter

Hiska Studio
annehawkinson@outlook.com
www.annehawkinson.com

First Printing, 2018
ISBN 978-1-7320175-0-4

Cover design by Damonza

Dedications

ANNE

To Nancy (my sister, my friend, my hero), bedtime reading, and libraries.

PAUL

To my mother and father, Margaret and Victor Hunter, and to the omnipresent child of wonder who resides within me.

Acknowledgements

Karey Anne, for her unending encouragement, support, and computer wizardry.

Our draft-readers, for taking time from their busy lives to spend it with our story.

Scotland - land of beauty, history, and tradition.

Chapter One

Maggie pulled the hood of her brown cloak over her long, auburn curls and shut the door behind her with a sigh. She paused for a moment, looking at the village she called home. Like a flower, Stonehaven unfurled from a central square with a deep, generous well at its heart. Rows of shops with homes above served the residents and farmers with a small stable, forge, and cowshed at one end. Aromas from the brewhouse and bakehouse three doors down filled the morning air. At the other end was a town hall, church, and the gently-swinging sign of the Thistle Top Inn.

With a parcel tucked under her arm, she stepped into the street on her way to Castle Wrought. William, one of the grooms at the castle, had brought the cloak to her family's shop for repair after it was torn by an agitated stallion. Until this morning, she'd managed to delay her father's request to return the mended cloak. She dreaded the crowds and commotion that were a part of everyday life there. "Can't you bring it? You'll be there Tuesday next."

"No, I told William you'd bring it today. Off you go then, lass."

Her life at nineteen was quieter since her mother's death three years ago. Cora was a devoted wife and mother and well-respected in Stonehaven. She worked alongside her husband Angus at The Weavers Hands where her warm generosity and genuine kindness transformed business acquaintances into friends. When the MacDonald family needed help during lambing season, Cora went to help without a moment's hesitation. She returned two days later, exhausted but happy and full of stories about the new lives they'd brought into the world.

Within a week, she had a fever. She tried to resume her duties in the shop and at home but when she collapsed outside the shop, Angus insisted she take to her bed. Maggie tended to her, and for a time it looked like she would recover. However, the next evening the fever came back with a vengeance. "Don't fuss over me," she whispered as Maggie wiped her glistening brow. Cora became delirious and then lost the ability to speak. When the pale light of dawn filled the room, she was gone. Maggie lay asleep on the floor next to her bed, unaware of her passing.

Maggie endured the small service and quiet burial in a stupor, paralyzed by grief. She knew they meant well, but cringed with each remark about the fact that she had her mother's eyes and beautiful hair. The townspeople praised Cora's generosity and willingness to help others – the very trait that took her life. It made her want to scream. Instead, she mumbled a polite response and slipped away as soon as she could.

Maggie wrestled with her anger and sorrow, gradually negotiating a truce that enabled her to move forward with her life. It had a new ebb and flow, and she found peace in its solitude. Her father had given up trying to find her a husband. She'd had suitors, and her father would have married her off to a rich spice merchant had she not hid in an abandoned cottage until the leering old man got tired of waiting and returned to London.

She kept to the side of the road, wading through the tall grass and avoiding the crowds, carts, and riders kicking up dust clouds as they galloped past. She wished she was walking west instead of north because the road west took her to the forest where she felt most at ease. She cherished her task of collecting the plants and berries that would dye the fabrics her father wove in his shop. It was something she and her mother had done often; picking what they needed and sharing lunch under the trees before heading back to the shop. Now, Maggie gathered alone and thought of her mother when she returned to their favorite spot near the river. She picked carefully and with respect, as her mother had taught her. When the basket was full, her time was her own.

She settled in a new spot – a fallen oak whose branches formed a rustic chair of sorts. From it, she watched the world around her come alive. Bees and butterflies went about their business, and a rabbit or squirrel might forage nearby. On more than one occasion, a deer made its way into the sun-dappled spot, knowing she was there. Their eyes met as she smiled and whispered, "I won't harm you."

Maggie stumbled on the hem of her cloak, bringing her back to the reality of life at Castle Wrought. She sighed with impatience at the congestion blocking the drawbridge and entrance to the castle courtyard. There was a cart with a broken wheel, another trying to get past, and people threading their way through the mess as they grumbled and pushed past the tired, old horse and its frustrated owner. She gave the horse the rest of her apple and a sympathetic pat as she entered the courtyard. The castle loomed up on three sides, circling the courtyard like massive grey arms.

Ancient stonework pushed into the sky - its crenellations reminded her of menacing teeth. Blue flags with white, x-shaped crosses snapped in the wind from their strategic locations high above the castle walls. Stone archways beyond the courtyard led to workrooms, the blacksmith, and the stables.

She assumed the stairs under the clock tower that led to the next level must be for merchants and servants. She'd only been up them once as a wee toddler with her father. He stood talking to a potential customer too long for her busy mind and body. She saw a fuzzy puppy run past the doorway, followed it down the stairs, and was immediately swept up in the tangle of people arriving for a special event. Maggie remembered being knocked down and no one stopping to help her up. She cried for her father, but no one seemed to notice until a familiar face bent over and loving hands scooped her up. It was Ida, the seamstress who owned the shop across the street from The Weavers Hands. She ignored the fact that Maggie had wet herself as she marched up the stairs to tell her father she'd be taking her home. Maggie buried her face in the folds of Ida's woolen cloak and fell asleep on the walk back to Stonehaven. She never wanted to go near the castle again.

Ida came to the shop the next morning with a beautiful doll. It was made of soft ivory muslin and had deep red hair and brown eyes, just like Maggie's. Her dress was dark green velvet with lace at the collar and hem. "Remnants from a castle order," she whispered to Cora. "Her name is Bridget," Ida said with a smile to Maggie as she handed her the doll. "She is your friend to take with you when you visit the castle. You can keep each other safe."

On the next trip and countless others that followed, Maggie made the trip to the castle with Bridget clutched tightly in her arms. She reluctantly left her behind when she grew too old to be seen with a doll. Maggie bought a small, wicker chair from Ewan Wood's shop at the end of the street for her worn and much-loved Bridget and placed her next to the window in her bedroom.

She thought about Bridget as she continued through the courtyard and imagined her hidden under her cloak. The smell of baking bread drifted on the wind, mixed with the aroma of roasting meat. *Probably wild boar*, she thought. Farmers filled their wooden stands with carrots, potatoes, and new lettuce to sell. A tinker and his cart settled into a corner to set up shop. A woodsmith set out a beautiful spinning wheel along with an assortment of bowls, stools, and chairs. It was a chaotic, happy setting. Instead of relaxing, her body grew tense; she felt eyes upon her as she made her way toward the stables. She glanced out from under her hood, but no one met her frightened gaze as she hurried to meet William.

***

He saw her hand, white as ivory, her long, slender fingers clutching her hood against the wind. Tendrils of deep red escaped, pulled free by a sudden gust. Then, she was gone. Lennox Brodie grunted under his breath, turned heel, and crossed the courtyard in the opposite direction. He was a tall, dark knight with wild hair and eyes to match. Clad in black from boots to cloak, those in his path gave a wide berth to his imposing presence. "Excuse me, Sir Brodie." "Begging your pardon, Sir Brodie." He nodded in silent, frowning acknowledgement, his cloak billowing as he climbed the stairs leading to the stonemason's shop.

Gathered in clusters below, the townspeople spoke in whispers about the knight with the tortured countenance, recently returned from fighting and hard-won battles. "Did you see the scar?" one asked. "He's inherited his father-in-law's lands and is building a manor house in the middle of it, away from everyone," said another. "You'd never know by looking at him that he used to be happy. He's changed and not for the better."

Her delivery to William complete, Maggie quickly crossed the courtyard behind two women, their conversation floating to her on the cool, May breeze. At first, she dismissed it as idle chatter, but when they spoke of the woods she listened intently. Someone by the name of Brodie buried his wife and two daughters there, killed by the famine six years ago. "Crazed with grief," one said. "Wouldn't bring them to the church or let the priest near them. Buried them with his own two hands somewhere in the woods – the property belongs to him now."

"People say he lives like a wild animal, though he dresses well and seems clean enough," the other said. "They say he's reckless and violent. Doesn't care whether he lives or dies. Hunters have seen him in the forest, wandering on foot or riding that black stallion of his at all hours - even when the weather is at its worst."

The women stopped at a vegetable stall to look over the last of the winter radishes and spring's first asparagus, and Maggie hurried past them. She was anxious to get back to Stonehaven, the security of the shop, and their home above it. What bothered her more was what she'd heard about the man visiting the forest. Who was this man, Brodie? The possibility of encountering him frightened her.

The forest was her sanctuary, her escape. She didn't want anyone taking that from her. The vastness of the forests surrounding Stonehaven reassured her. She hadn't seen him since his return and probably never would.

Chapter Two

Lennox Brodie meant to die. He wanted to die. He railed against God for sparing him. "Why? Why?" he screamed at the black, starlit sky, seeking answers that never came. When heartbreak and exhaustion overtook him, he fell asleep next to the grave, the cold mist settling on him like a mourner's shroud. He left the next morning for Jerusalem - an angry, grief-stricken knight with an empty soul. The Holy Wars would fulfill his oath to the king, and he was ready to fight and kill.

He returned two years later, scarred and wealthy, but still without a soul. On the journey home, he broke away from the returning column to visit the grave of his wife and young daughters. Lennox leapt from the saddle and ran to the grave, tearing at the weeds and small saplings that dared take root in his absence. He left the primrose, heather, and a clump of thistles to hug the side of the stone. Bowing his head in a whispered a prayer of remembrance, he apologized for the simple stone bearing only their first names – Elizabeth, Rose, and Anna. At the time it was all he could afford. He had money now. Perhaps he'd have a new, proper stone made.

Lennox stood with a sigh, surveying the lands that were left to him upon the death of his father-in-law. They adjoined the vast holdings of his father - now his as well. He would build a home here, away from human contact. Titus, his black Friesian, would have a fine stable with room for the colts and fillies he'd sire. That's what Lennox loved now, what kept what was left of his heart alive - horses.

The days were easier than the nights. Lennox kept himself busy during the day helping to clear the land or traveling between the castle and Stonehaven to meet with carpenters, glass makers, and stonemasons. When night fell, the demons of his past came calling. The first time he woke up screaming, his servant Darby burst into the room armed with a candlestick, ready to defend his master. When a flying boot grazed his shoulder and Lennox bellowed, "Get out!" Darby took to covering his ears at night and never speaking of it in the morning.

Lennox tried to keep the tortuous, haunting dreams at bay by drinking himself into a stupor that began late in the afternoon and continued well into the night. However, the anguish of his past was more powerful than the strongest ale or wine. He fought his battles over and over, seeing the eyes and souls of those he'd killed – men too old to be fighting, most his own age, and many too young to be on a battlefield. At the last, he'd see Elizabeth reaching her hand out to him. He would try to grasp it, but she was always just beyond his touch. As she faded from sight, he'd throw himself out of bed – arms reaching for her and calling her name.

He staggered to his feet amongst the shadows and stood in front of the oak table near the door. The solitary candle cast a dull light on the discolored, damaged corner that mirrored the injuries to his right hand and fist. It also illuminated his massive, two-handed sword that hung on the wall, unsheathed and ready at a moment's notice. It was once polished and oiled, the shining blade revealing its finely-etched filigree. The hilt's textured grip had long-since formed itself to Lennox's hand. It was dull and dusty now, but the blade retained its razor-sharp edge as well-made swords do.

Drenched in sweat, he pulled off his nightshirt and climbed back into bed, willing his heart to slow to its normal rhythm. Rubbing his fingers through his newly-trimmed beard, he stared at the sword, its presence a painful reminder of what he was and who he'd become. Its scabbard hung on a peg along with his surcoat - scraped, scarred, and battle-worn. The Brodie coat of arms of a hand gripping four arrows was frayed and stained by his life as a knight. The waist bore the permanent marking of leather belts cinched around it - the colors of red, black, and gold faded with age.

Lennox rolled over, turning his back on his sword and surcoat. He pulled the quilt over his now-chilled body, covered his ears against the screams of those he'd killed, and surrendered himself to the tears of sorrow that would eventually grant him an exhaustive sleep.

Chapter Three

"Take an extra basket with you, lass," Angus called over his shoulder. "One for the plants we need for dyes and one for whatever wildflowers are in bloom."

"Why am I gathering wildflowers?"

"You can tie them into bouquets and sell them at Market Day tomorrow. It is spring and the ladies at court will want fresh flowers in their sitting rooms."

"Can't you sell them? You'll be at your stall anyway," she argued. "I have things to do here."

"I have other business to conduct," he said. "And it will do you good to be around people."

"But…" Maggie protested.

"It's done then. I'll hear no more about it."

Maggie huffed in frustration, threw on her cloak, and closed the door behind her with enough force to rattle the glass in its frame.

"Mornin', Maggie!" Ida called as she swept the area outside the door of her shop. "Got time for a fresh-baked bannock?"

"Not today, sorry." Ida nodded as Maggie hurried down the street and followed the path leading to the forest. As she reached the stands of oak and pine, the anger she felt toward her father was nearly gone. Calmed by the cool canopy of the trees and the songs of the finches and sparrows, she set about gathering the madder, weld, and lichen. She took her time and gathered a few from each spot so they would have a chance to grow back.

Then she turned her attention to gathering flowers for the bouquets to sell at Market Day. She'd brought along her scissors and carefully clipped the bluebells, wood anemone, and lady's smock. At the edge of the pond, she noticed the fuzzy catkins on the pussy willows and added some to her basket.

A pair of chattering, red squirrels chased each other up a path Maggie had never taken. She followed them to the top of the hill where they scolded her from the branches of an aged pine. The trees opened into a sheltered clearing; when Maggie turned she saw the stone nestled under a flowering crab apple tree.

It was a simple, arched tablet of grey with three names carved on its surface:

Elizabeth
Rose
Anna

Maggie looked around. Satisfied that she was alone, she knelt next to the grave. It had recently been disturbed as though someone was tending it, but small pockets told her the squirrels had dug into its surface in their search for acorns buried there last fall. When she smoothed the earth back into place, her hand was poked by a sharp edge. It was a small, wooden cross; two more lay just under the surface. She held them in her hands - small bits of wood, bound with dark, human hair.

An unexpected wave of sadness washed over her, bringing with it the memory of the loss of her mother. She bowed her head in grief and loss. Quietly sobbing, her tears dripped onto the soft, fertile soil as her auburn tresses brushed the leaf-littered ground. Her sorrow released, she sat up and looked at the crosses again, suddenly feeling like an intruder in someone's sacred, private place.

Then she remembered the conversation she'd overheard. Could this be the grave the women in the courtyard spoke of? The wife and children buried by Lennox the knight? Heart pounding in fear, she pulled back the earth and replaced the crosses. After covering them, she picked a sprig of anemone and placed it next to the stone. She hurried down the hill, retrieved her basket, and ran out of the forest.

Chapter Four

Market Day at the castle was a social event as well as an opportunity to buy and sell. It felt like the entire town of Stonehaven was in attendance along with the families from the farms and outlying areas. The courtyard was choked with vendors and shoppers, shouting and laughing as they jostled baskets and boxes among the stalls draped with striped or patterned awnings.

Cattle and sheep were herded through the walkways, leaving steamy droppings on their way to the holding pens. Chickens squawked in their cages, followed by honking geese and the barking dogs that chased them. At the far end of the courtyard, the food vendors were set up, selling roast pork and chicken, baked bannocks, and the first rowan berries of the season.

Maggie was alone and grateful to be standing behind the table, out of the crush of people. Her father had stepped away to visit the stall of a friend; Maggie wished he'd hurry back and hoped no one would visit their stall until he did. The feeling of unease and panic never left her in settings like these. The trauma related to her visit so many years ago had grown into a dislike of crowds, noise, and the chaos that came along with it. She repositioned the bouquets she'd made in the bucket of water and added several more from the one behind her.

As she finished tying a red ribbon around a cluster of lady's smock, the sense of being watched settled over her. She glanced up without raising her head and saw him – tall and muscular, dressed in black, and watching her from across the walkway. The feeling of panic welled up as she stepped to the far end of the table and the colorful bolts of fabric; she busied herself unfolded and re-folded them. A servant laden with the day's purchases selected a bolt of soft, green wool. As she completed the transaction, he walked up to her.

Maggie took a deep breath and squared her shoulders. She looked up at him, her brown eyes meeting his almost-black and tried to ignore the pulse pounding in her ears. Lennox wrung his gloves in his hands, suddenly tongue-tied and nervous. He finally managed to croak, "The one with the red bow."

"Yes, sir." She rushed to finish the purchase, anxious to have him gone and away from her. As she handed him the bouquet, her hair tangled in the ribbon.

"Sorry, sir," she said, her cheeks flushing with embarrassment.

As he opened his mouth to speak, he was bumped from behind by a small girl, laughing and running ahead of her father. His quick reflexes stopped her from falling, but when he straightened and faced Maggie, his face was tight with tension and his jaw clenched in intense, emotional pain. He tossed a handful of coins into the basket, snatched the flowers from her hand, and turned to leave.

"Beggin' yer pardon, Sir Brodie. The wee lass…" The rest of his apology fell on deaf ears as the knight elbowed his way through the crowd and out of sight.

"Who was that?" Maggie asked the girl's father.

"That, mistress, was Sir Lennox Brodie."

Maggie's hand trembled as she took the money from the basket and put it into her pocket. The coins were still warm from the heat of his hand. He was the knight she'd overheard the two women speaking about - the knight who'd buried his wife and daughters in the grave in the woods.

Outside the gates, Lennox took Titus' reins from the groom, swung into the black leather saddle, and tucked the flowers into his tunic. He spurred Titus to a gallop harder than he meant, and Titus responded by throwing his head and pulling at the bit. Lennox apologized as he calmed the angry stallion and slowed him to a walk once they'd turned onto the west road. The ride through the open, breezy meadows gave him time to think about the young woman who'd transformed him from confident knight to bashful youth with just a glance.

He'd watched her from a distance, gradually moving closer to the stall where she was working. He was physically attracted to her auburn hair, the curve of her neck, and the graceful hands he was sure he'd seen the other day. There was something about her that set her apart from the other pretty women vying for his attention. She had a gentleness about her, a tenderness in the way she touched the flowers or tied a ribbon. There was something more than physical beauty about her, and he wanted to know it.

He let Titus graze untethered when they reached the grave; he was well-trained and wouldn't wander far. Kneeling over the mound of earth, he smoothed and patted it gently before placing the flowers on it. He pulled a tangled strand of auburn hair from the ribbon, smiling as he remembered how it had happened. Bowing his head, he recited his prayer of remembrance. As he crossed himself and prepared to rise, the sun glinted on another strand of red. He pulled it from the leaves next to the grave, instantly knowing who it belonged to.

A tumble of conflicting emotions flooded Lennox's heart and soul. His initial anger at someone trespassing on his land and intruding on its sacred space dissolved like the sun on the morning mist when he realized who the visitor was. This was the grave of his wife and daughters; smiling and thinking of the young maiden who visited here seemed disloyal and blasphemous. She had roused feelings in him that he thought were dead forever. After all he'd done and the man he had become, did he have the capacity to love? Even if he did, there was no guarantee his feelings would be returned. "She'd never come to love anyone like me," he whispered to Titus, leaning his head against the stallion's cheek. He climbed up and galloped for home, seeking the promise of oblivion that lay at the bottom of a bottle of wine.

Chapter Five

Lennox woke up in a pile of leaf litter under a sycamore, twisted and sore. His head pounded as he stood to relieve himself, a cruel reminder of last night's miserable attempt to escape his past and the dreams that haunted him. Terror-filled eyes of men meeting their death at his hand flooded his sleeping mind along with the whimpering resignation of the women he'd violated out of anger-fueled lust. Then there were the children. He'd awakened before that dream had a chance to torture him once again.

The cold water of the stream revived him as he splashed it onto his face and drank from cupped hands, chasing the taste of stale wine from his mouth. Droplets fell from his beard as he stood, alerted by an unfamiliar sound. Cocking his head, his ears strained to hear what he thought was a woman singing. He scrambled up the bank and crept to the edge of the hill that overlooked the sun-dappled glade. Crawling behind a fallen oak, he peered over the edge. She was there.

He watched as she braided her hair. Her hands gently guided each strand into place, securing it at the end with a blue ribbon. She sang a song whose tune was familiar to him, the words faded long ago from his memory. The woman continued to sing as she filled her basket. Lennox watched, feeling guilty about spying on her but not guilty enough to leave.

When she glanced in his direction, he ducked down and held his breath as he prayed to the damp soil that she didn't discover him. From a space under the trunk, he watched her walk to the edge of the path leading to the grave. She took a step, hesitated as she looked around, and then turned away. She appeared uneasy as she took her basket and followed the path out of the woods.

Lennox was careful not to follow her too closely. He'd learned to stalk prey in the woods and catch enemies unaware in the wars he fought. He knew how to remain hidden while keeping her in sight. He followed from a safe distance on the opposite side of the lane, ducking into a shop doorway when he heard someone called her name – Maggie.

She stopped at the entrance to The Weavers Hands. Maggie didn't appear happy to see the man approaching her and took several steps backward. Lennox recognized Lyle de Mortimer at once by his wiry stature, copper-colored hair, and the limp he'd earned as a young boy after falling from a horse. He took Maggie's hand and leaned in to kiss both cheeks, lingering too long on each of them. Maggie pulled away with a nervous smile, saying something he couldn't hear. Keeping her basket between them, she entered the shop and closed the door behind her.

Lennox waited where he was, a sentinel of sorts, until Lyle turned away and was out of sight. The need to protect her was an odd feeling, but it warmed a small corner of his heart and made him feel more like a man than feral beast. He retraced his steps and returned to the forest with his thoughts. When he came to the edge of the path leading to the grave, he decided on a plan to make his presence known.

Leaving the ale on the table untouched, Lennox spent the evening polishing the silver spurs left to him by his father. He gave special attention to the letter "B" engraved on its shank, hoping she would connect it to his surname of Brodie and encourage her to seek him out to return the "lost" item. He chose one and set it on the table by the door. As he set it down, he traced his fingers on the table's damaged corner without feeling the need to take his fist to it.

He lay in bed, studying the sword on the wall with less disgust and self-loathing than he had on previous nights. The haunting dreams still came, but Lennox fought them off and spent the rest of the night pacing back and forth, unable to sleep. He prayed for forgiveness, explaining and justifying his actions to himself and the silent furnishings surrounding him. With the first blush in the eastern sky, he pulled on his trousers, boots, and swung his cloak over his shoulders against the early morning chill. He gave the spur a kiss for luck and crossed the clearing that led to the forest.

Titus whinnied in his stall, voicing his displeasure at being left behind. Lennox shushed him, entered the forest, and stopped at the grave. He knelt and bowed his head as he recited his prayer of remembrance. As he crossed himself, he whispered his intent and begged for their acceptance and blessing. He hurried down the hill, slipping and sliding on the wet leaves, avoiding the path itself and the telltale boot marks he'd leave going down. He dropped the spur in the middle of the path's entrance to make it appear as an accident and then stepped into the glade where he could see it from where Maggie might come upon it. Satisfied, he walked up the path and purposely left footprints, his heart pounding with more than exertion.

Chapter Six

It was late morning by the time Maggie arrived at the glade. The shop was busy with customers placing and picking up orders and browsers who weren't sure what they wanted. Lyle had come in, acting like a gentleman when Maggie's father was in the room. The moment her father left, Lyle backed her into a corner for a kiss. She pushed him away and moved past him, but he grabbed her arm, insulted at her rejection. "I'll have you, Maggie, one way or the other."

"Leave me alone, Lyle. I don't have feelings for you, so please go and stay away," she whispered to avoid calling attention to herself by the patrons in the shop. She walked with forced calmness behind the counter to help a customer, and Lyle left when her father returned.

When the last customer left the shop, she bade her father goodbye and hurried out the back door. Maggie glanced over her shoulder several times on the way to the forest, but there was no sign of Lyle. She sighed with relief as she stepped into the glade. Laying her cloak on the rustic chair, she extended her arms and turned in a slow, dancing circle lit by a shaft of the sun. The beauty and peace erased the unpleasant encounter with Lyle, and Maggie hummed and sang as she gathered the plants and tree bark her father needed.

Her basket full, Maggie leaned back in her chair to savor a bit of grana cheese and oatmeal bread. She threw tiny bits to the sparrow foraging next to a tree; when a gust of wind shifted its branches, it cast a stream of light onto an object in the path leading to the grave she'd discovered on her last visit. As she reached to pick it up, she noticed the footprints leading up the hill toward the grave. The spur was costly - silver, engraved with a filigree "B" in the center of the shaft. Lennox Brodie. The spur must belong to him. She followed the tracks past the grave, crested the hill, and looked across the clearing.

At the far end was a small structure, dwarfed by the skeleton of a huge manor house under construction. The front faced a vast, grassy meadow while the back hugged the edge of the forest. *It's as they said*, she thought. She didn't dare venture near the house, but laid the spur on the grave next to the flowers he'd purchased from her on Market Day. He'd find it on his next visit. With a glance over her shoulder, she retrieved her cloak and basket and left the forest for home.

***

Lennox spent most of the next morning at Castle Wrought reviewing the next phase of construction with the stonemason. He struggled to concentrate on the reference drawings placed on the table in front of him. His mind pictured Maggie smiling and holding his spur instead of the next wall to be erected. He forced himself to concentrate, hurried down the stairs, and let Titus have free reign to gallop back to the forest. He slid from the black-studded saddle, glanced at the grave in passing, and stopped short. His spur was there, next to the flowers. When had she come? Was she still here? He snatched it up, hurried to the edge of the hill, and looked down. His chest was tight and his heart pounding when he saw her in the glade below.

Her green frock followed her curves; her auburn locks were loose and flowing. She hummed as she set her basket down and saw him standing on the hill above her. Maggie's expression changed from one of happiness to fright as she hurriedly gathered her things and began to back away.

"Wait!" he called. "A moment, please." He walked down the path, trying not to hurry or appear too eager. He approached her and bowed. "I am Sir Lennox Brodie."

"I'm Maggie Weaver, sir. If you'll excuse me, I'll be leaving now."

"Please, wait. The spur – did you place it on the grave?" He held it out for her to see.

"I did. I thought it belonged to you. Was I mistaken?"

"No, it belongs to me. I must have dropped it along the way. Thank you for returning it." He paused, feeling awkward and unfamiliar in a position to atone for his behavior. "I want to apologize for my actions at the market the other day. It was unacceptable. Will you forgive me?" Lennox was relieved to see her relax and smile.

"I will," she laughed quietly. "The crowds and chaos sometimes bring out the worst in people. I much prefer being here."

"Aye, I agree." He shifted from one foot to the other and looked around. "Do you know who owns these lands?"

"Stuart Campbell, sir. He granted my father permission to gather what we need for our cloth dyes from these woods."

Lennox hesitated before responding. He didn't want to alarm her. "Actually, these lands are mine. The Campbell lands begin at the ridge north of where we're standing."

Maggie's face went white with fright. "I'm sorry, sir. I didn't know…" She clutched her things tighter to her chest and backed away towards the path.

"Please, mistress." He held his hand out to her – an odd sensation. "I only meant to tell you so you would know that you have my permission to roam any parts of the lands that are mine in search of your plants and such. No one will turn you out. If they do, send word to me at once."

"Thank you. It's very kind of you, sir." She gave him a nervous, but grateful smile. "I must be going now. Thank you again for your kindness."

"You're most welcome - perhaps we shall meet again."

"Perhaps." Maggie looked down, cheeks flushing. "Good day to you, sir."

"Good day, Mistress Maggie." He watched her leave the forest, her cloak fastened and hood covering her head. He didn't realize how hard he'd been clutching the spur and rubbed at the dent in his palm. He tossed it happily in the air as he ambled up the path. Then something unexpected happened – something he hadn't done in years. He laughed out loud.

Chapter Seven

Lennox began taking daily rides through his lands, making sure he was near the glade or nearby woods when he thought Maggie might be there. His heart sank when the rain kept her away or he came upon her as she was leaving, but she'd turn and wave if he called her name. Sometimes he'd stop and visit; other times he'd watch her from a distance, not wanting to disturb her or appear too intrusive. He felt protective of her. She was on the lands he owned, and it was his duty to keep her safe. Never mind the fact that he was falling in love with her.

He stopped at the grave and offered his prayer of remembrance. The need of a daily visit had diminished, and he felt a sense of acceptance that his wife and daughters had given him their blessing to move on and find love again. The dreams continued, but not as often, and Lennox grew less dependent on the wine's ability to help him endure the terrors of the night.

He visited The Weavers Hands to introduce himself to Maggie's father and inquire about the woven goods he'd need for his new home. It was also a perfect excuse to see

Maggie; she looked up and smiled when he came through the door. "Good Morning, Mistress Maggie," he said with a nod, returning the smile. "Is your father in? I'd like a word with him."

"This way, sir." She led him to a room at the back of the shop. He couldn't help but watch the way her body moved under her lavender gown, and the draft created by her steps carried with it the scent of sweet and spice.

"Will you be visiting the glade tomorrow?" he asked in a hushed voice.

"I believe so. Sometime in the late morning after the dew has dried," she whispered. She stood to the side while her father and Lennox exchanged introductions, then turned and left the room. It was hard to concentrate, knowing Maggie was mere steps away. He forced himself to focus on the conversation with Angus, the decisions to be made, and the feeling of elation knowing return visits would be necessary.

Lennox returned to the front of the shop and found Lyle de Mortimer leaning over the counter, whispering something to Maggie and letting his eyes rest on parts of her body that forced Maggie to grab her shawl and cover herself. Lennox's protective hackles rose as he stepped between Lyle and the counter. "Are you here to make a purchase?" he asked Lyle, using his height, build, and dark anger to his advantage.

"I'm thinking about something I want," he answered, looking around Lennox at Maggie.

"There is nothing here for you," Lennox growled. Lyle backed away in tandem with Lennox's forward steps, limping and stumbling as he reached the door. Lennox closed it firmly and returned to Maggie. "Are you alright? He didn't hurt you, did he?"

"No, I'm fine, thank you," she answered, relieved at Lyle's departure. "He's very persistent and won't take 'no' for an answer. He frightens me with his forward ways and vulgar words."

"Rest easy, Maggie. I shall watch over you and keep you from harm."

"Thank you, sir. That puts my mind at ease."

"Please, call me Lennox."

"Oh, I couldn't! It would be disrespectful for me to address you that way."

Lennox laughed. "I understand your concern. Perhaps when it's just the two of us you'll reconsider?"

"Aye, I'll reconsider," she said with a smile, her brown eyes sparkling with happiness. A customer in the shop needing assistance called to her. "I'm sorry, you must excuse me."

"Until tomorrow," Lennox said with a bow.

"Tomorrow," Maggie whispered as she moved past him.

Chapter Eight

Lennox hovered and paced in the kitchen, its rough-hewn beams and wooden chopping block made from trees felled on his land. Tall, wooden shelves were full to nearly bursting with crockery, plates, and cooking vessels. Clay pots of rosemary and thyme leaned toward the light in the east-facing windows as if watching the herd of cows grazing near the hillside. The aroma of rye bread wafted through the kitchen and beyond, making Lennox impatient and anxious to be on his way.

Corliss slapped his hand away as he peeked into the domed oven, then took the loaves out and set them on their sides to cool. The tiny, grey-haired woman was more of a mother to him than a kitchen servant and had been a part of the Brodie household since his infancy. "Would you care to explain why I'm packing extra food and *two* goblets?" She turned to him with raised eyebrows and sparkling, blue eyes as she added edam cheese, fresh-picked strawberries, and two bottles of cider to the basket.

"No, I wouldn't," Lennox laughed. "And I'll thank you to keep it to yourself," he whispered, hugging her as he took the sturdy willow basket, two fruit tarts, and left the kitchen.

"Here! Take this throw with you," she called, running after him. "Can't have the lass sittin' on the bare, damp ground." Lennox laid the plaid tartan in the Brodie colors of red, black, and gold across Titus' withers and galloped across the clearing to the forest. He bowed with respect when he passed the grave and eagerly looked for Maggie when he reached the edge of the hill overlooking the glade. It was empty, but Lennox was sure she'd come today. He went down the hill and looked for a suitable spot for them to share the lunch he'd brought. Along the way, he found an early blooming rose and picked it for her.

He set the basket on the rustic chair and turned to see her entering the forest. She smiled when she saw him; he watched her graceful hands as she lowered the hood of her cloak. He took one and kissed it. "Greetings, Maggie. I'm happy to see you." She blushed when he released her hand and gave her the rose.

"Thank you, sir…" she started to say.

"Remember, you agreed to call me Lennox when it's just the two of us."

"Aye, Lennox it shall be, when it's just the two of us."

"I brought some lunch, but perhaps you need to gather your plants and things first."

"Yes, that might be best." They walked together through the forest and low-lying areas, Maggie naming the various plants and their uses as she filled her basket. "Some of these may be used on the materials for your order," she laughed. When they returned to the glade, Lennox spread the tartan throw on the ground for them to sit on. He unwrapped the bread, cheese, and fruit and filled her goblet with cider. They both grew quiet, feeling awkward and unsure of what to say.

"Thank you for this," Maggie said. "It was very thoughtful."

"Was nothing. Just a wee lunch, that's all." He took a sip from his goblet as he watched her hair catch in the breeze, laughing as she tried to get it under control.

"I should have braided it," she said, laughing along with him.

"It's beautiful no matter what you do with it – beautiful, like the rest of you."

"Please, you're too kind," she replied quietly as she bowed her head, her cheeks turning a soft pink. She toyed with a blade of grass, twisting it around her finger. Then she looked up, her brown eyes meeting his. "So, tell me about yourself. I don't know anything about you except what you told me on our walk."

Lennox told her what he could without going into the most painful parts of his past. Since she'd already seen and visited the grave, he told her about his wife and daughters. He spoke of his love of horses and the stable he was building to raise the offspring his stallion Titus would sire. When she questioned the scar on his cheek, he told her it was a result of fighting in Jerusalem, nothing more. He hadn't resolved the conflicted feelings of shame and pride haunting his past. Until he did, those feelings would be kept covered and hidden.

"And you?" he asked, anxious to change the subject. "I know your father is a weaver and importer of fabrics and other goods, and you work in his shop. But that's all I know."

"There's not much to tell. I'm an only child - my mother died three years ago. I live a quiet life helping my father. My greatest joy is being here in the woods – it's so quiet and peaceful, nothing like the chaos at the castle or the people of Stonehaven who are always meddling in your personal business." She looked down, hesitant about her next words. "Please don't think I've gone soft in the head, but sometimes I hear voices when I'm here – like the plants or animals are speaking to me, or to each other." Lennox smiled at this, and Maggie was immediately embarrassed. "I should never have told you."

"No, I'm glad you did. I believe you. The forest is a living, breathing place as much as the creatures that call it home. I don't think everyone can hear them. I can't, or at least I never have. I think it's a special person who connects with nature, cares for it, and respects it. You have a gift, Maggie."

"I'm not so sure, but thank you."

They grew more comfortable in each other's company as the afternoon sun shifted in the glade. They shared stories of their youth, likes and dislikes, and their thoughts about the world around them. His fear of spiders made her smile. "A strong, brave knight like you, afraid of a spider?"

Lennox laughed. "I can't really explain it, but I am." He leaned toward her and whispered, "Perhaps you can help me overcome my fear, but it must remain a secret or I'll never be able to show my face again."

"Your secret is safe with me," she grinned.

"I believe that. I don't trust many people, but I trust you, Maggie."

A distant rumble of thunder caused her to look up at the sky. "It's getting late, and I must get back before I get caught in the rain." She stood, put on her cloak, and settled its hood in place. "Thank you for your company and for the lunch. It was wonderful. Truly."

Lennox stood as well, towering over her as he straightened to his full height. He put the remains of their lunch in the basket and shook the leaves and twigs from the throw. "We'll do it again if you like."

"I would, thank you." Then she sighed and picked up her basket. "And now I must go."

Lennox walked her to the edge of the forest. He took her hand and kissed it, her skin soft and warm against his lips. "Be safe, Mistress Maggie." He watched her leave, returning her wave before she slipped from his sight.

They met often in the forest in the days and weeks that followed, walking together or sitting in a sheltered spot, talking for hours about everything and nothing.

On a warm Saturday in June, Maggie brought a lunch of meat pies, raspberry tarts, and cider that they shared on the bank of a stream on Lennox's property.

Lennox purposely chose the secluded spot, guiding Titus far from the glade or prying eyes. Maggie was mindful to bring her gathering basket and quickly filled it so that the rest of the afternoon could be spent with Lennox. After eating and casual conversation, they laid back on the soft, thick grass in the dappled shade. Their voices quieted to whispers, speaking of feelings and each other, not things. Tentative kisses grew more intense and passionate as the afternoon wore on.

His breath was heavy in her hair. "I love you, Maggie. I love you. Do you hear me?" When she nodded, he asked with fear pounding in his heart, "Do you think you could find it in your heart to love me?" When he heard her whispered 'yes', he tightened his embrace and kissed her deeply and thoroughly. "I never thought I'd say those words again, much less have someone say they love me in return."

Maggie took his face in hers and looked into his eyes. "I love you, Lennox. Now there can be no doubt." She pulled his mouth to hers, and Lennox felt himself harden. It was then that he that finally pulled back.

"I want you, Maggie. I want to love you the way a man loves a woman. But I want to be honorable. I haven't

been honorable towards women in a very long time.
You've made me want to be a better man. And taking you
here is not the way I want us to come together." He shifted
his arm so her head rested on it. "I'm willing to wait until
the time is right. Can you accept that and save yourself for
me?"

Maggie smiled and kissed the top of his hand. "I am
yours, Lennox Brodie. I'll never give myself to anyone but
you." Reluctantly, they gathered their things, and Lennox
lifted her onto Titus with a kiss. She rode with her head
resting against Lennox's back, his warm strength and male
scent intoxicating as anything she could imagine.

Maggie and Lennox chose to keep their feelings for
each other away from prying eyes and wagging tongues.
They avoided Stonehaven, where people would watch and
gossip and where Maggie was afraid of encountering Lyle.
Lennox felt protective of her and preferred to keep her out
of the gaze of the workmen and the household servants who
meant well, but would find it hard to contain their
happiness when they saw the reason for the welcome
change in their master's demeanor.

Lennox often thought about the afternoon by the
river and knew he'd done the right thing in restraining his

urges. He hadn't always acted with honor, and part of him felt shame in the way he'd taken women out of blind, lustful need when he was away fighting in Jerusalem, Spain, and North Africa. Those times were behind him now - there was something special about Maggie that made him want to be a better man, to court her the way she deserved, and to build a relationship that would stand the test of time. He knew she was worth the wait.

Chapter Nine

Maggie was disappointed, but smiled at the comfort and security of their relationship. Lennox was having Titus re-shod at the castle and would not be meeting her that day. She pulled her cloak tighter against the chilly, June wind. Rain clouds were building in the west, so she planned to make a quick trip of picking the weld and lichen her father needed.

As she walked along the edge of the stream, she noticed a doe standing on the opposite bank. She crouched to make herself smaller and not frighten her. Their eyes met, and she spoke softly to the shy creature, its ears alert and listening. "I won't hurt you, beautiful girl." It watched her a moment longer, then lowered its head to drink. Maggie looked at her own reflection in the water and smiled at the serene happiness Lennox's affection had given her.

A reflected face emerged from over her shoulder. The startled doe looked up and bolted into the woods, her white tail signaling danger. It wasn't Lennox's face; it was Lyle's, with a leering smile, then a darting tongue. Maggie gasped, turning around as she stood up, but she was alone. A gust of wind caught the hood of her cloak as if it were pushing her out of the woods. The trees whispered to her – *leave, hurry.*

She left the stream, climbed the bank, and rushed to where she knew she could quickly gather the lichen she needed. The mature oaks grew at the edge of the glade where she and Lennox usually met. Her fingers trembled as she peeled away the lichen - she was anxious to be done and on her way.

As Maggie dropped the last bit into her basket and turned to leave, she came face-to-face with Lyle de Mortimer. "In a hurry, lass?" Maggie gasped with surprise and fear and tried to step around him.

"Yes, I am, so let me pass. My father is expecting me."

Instead of backing away, Lyle moved close enough for Maggie to smell his foul breath and body odor. She turned her head aside, but Lyle grabbed her jaw and yanked it back to face him. "I've been watching your comings and goings for a while, wondering what you're doing on lands that Lennox claims belong to him. Gone sweet on him, have ye?" His lips curled back, revealing decayed and missing teeth.

Maggie watched the saliva ooze out of an empty spot onto his chin. "How dare you spy on me!" she snapped. "I'll have you know I have permission to gather what I need from these lands and that's all I'm doing - not that it's any of your concern. Now, let go of me." She tried to wrench her arm free, but Lyle tightened his painful grip.

"Aye, I'll let you go, but not just yet," he whispered, pulling the basket from her hands and tossing it aside. "We've a little business of our own to conduct first." Lyle reached around Maggie, and before she realized what was happening, he'd lashed her wrists together with a leather strap. Having her under his control reminded him of when, as a young boy, he tied a kitten to a tree and shot it with arrows. He decided to kill it because it scratched and bit him when he tossed it into the air while trying to play with it. The kitten struggled and cried as Maggie was doing now. Lyle savored the feeling of power it gave him - having total control over another human being. He dragged her to a small tree and tied the ends of the strap around it, anchoring her to the ground in front of him – fitting, as he remembered the kitten. He wouldn't kill her, but he'd make her pay for her rejection of him. He wanted the kitten to love him, and it had hurt him instead. The same was true of Maggie.

Lyle had known her since he was a wee lad. He was drawn to her kind and gentle nature, something he had never felt in his own family. He loved her brown eyes and auburn hair, her happy laugh and giving ways. She'd included him in games of tug-of-war and leapfrog with the other children so he wouldn't feel left out. It was his eyes that scared the other children and made their parents pull them away from him. One was blue, the other green, like his father's. No one dared say anything when he was with him, but on his own he was teased and bullied. When Maggie defended him, the boys turned on her, taunting her with chants of, "Maggie loves Lyle." Lyle was secretly proud of their chants. Someday it would be true, and she would be his.

Then it happened – the autumn he turned fourteen, when Maggie and a group of her friends were picking apples in the orchard. He limped over to talk to her, telling her about his riding accident. Her eyes grew soft with concern, and she touched his arm in sympathy. Lyle misread her concern for love. His teenage lust took control, and he pulled her to him in an awkward, rough kiss. He pushed her up against the tree, kissing her as he ran his hands over her breasts, traveling down until he found the spot between her legs.

He could not have foreseen what happened next. She'd always been so kind to him; never had an angry word passed between them. Surely, she felt the same about him as he did toward her. He couldn't have been more wrong. Maggie pushed him away and slapped his cheek. "How dare you, Lyle! I thought you were my friend!"

"I am your friend, Maggie, but I want us to be more than friends. I love you, and I want you to be mine and mine alone. I want us to be married someday."

"No, Lyle. We were never more than friends, and you've just destroyed that. From now on, I want you to stay away from me. Stay away, and leave me alone." She took her basket, ran to join her friends, and left the orchard. In the months and years that followed, Lyle tried to make amends, but Maggie refused to forgive him and spoke in cool, polite formalities when it was impossible to avoid him.

It had taken years, but she was his now, to do with as he pleased. He would finish what he started that day in

the orchard. He would have her any way he wanted.
Maggie screamed and kicked wildly, prompting Lyle to
stuff a filthy rag in her mouth. He stood back, rubbing the
growing bulge in his trousers, looking down at her. "So…
where to start?"

He straddled her, pulled the rag from her mouth,
and kissed her forcefully, his coarse beard scratching her
soft, tender skin. Maggie bit his tongue when he forced it
into her mouth; he pulled back and slapped her on one
cheek, then the other. "You want to bite, do you? Well,
you're not the only one who knows how to bite."

He pulled his knife from its sheath, slit the laces of
Maggie's corset, and ripped her shift down the front. The
rag was jammed back in, and Lyle began at Maggie's neck,
kissing and biting while he crudely squeezed her breasts.
"Nice and soft, just as I imagined," he said, sucking and
pulling on each one. Maggie's eyes widened in pain but she
blinked back the tears – she wouldn't give Lyle the
satisfaction of seeing her cry. Her eyes traveled up the tree
trunk to a raven that had just landed on one of the
uppermost branches. It squawked loudly as if calling for
help.Fearing what might come next, Maggie squeezed her
legs together with all of the strength she could muster, but

it wasn't enough. Lyle pulled her skirt up over her waist and pried

her legs open with one knee, then the other. He fumbled with his trousers, struggling to pull them down with one hand, the other reaching for her crotch. He leaned up and looked at her. "Now, I expected you to be all wet and ready for me – do I have to do everything?" Lyle spat into his hand and smeared it between her legs. "The wait is finally over, 'cause your maidenhead is mine."

Maggie had no way to prepare for what followed. Lyle rammed himself inside her, grinding in and out, his hands on her bruising breasts. She gasped and moaned in pain, but she was certain Lyle didn't hear her over his panting and grunting. Mating animals were gentler. His mouth hung open, tongue darting in and out like a snake's, dripping saliva on her neck and chest as he pumped back and forth above her.

She arched her neck away from his dripping tongue and rancid breath. Desperate for any distraction, her eyes traveled up the height of the tree and locked onto those of the raven watching her from its perch. Her mind detached itself from her body, carrying her back to when she was a wee girl running with her terrier, Shamus, in a field of wildflowers. She was on a picnic with her parents in a high meadow overlooking Stonehaven. The sun warmed her face, the scent of the heather filled the air, and Shamus' happy yips made her smile and laugh as she fell and he leapt into her arms. She rolled over and over down a gentle slope, just as she was rolling now. Shamus was tugging on her hair. But wait. It wasn't Shamus.

It was Lyle with a handful, yanking it and bringing her back to reality. "Look at me! I want you to remember that it was me who had you first. I want you to remember it for the rest of your life." His lust-distorted face quivered as it hovered inches above hers. Maggie looked into his eyes. For an instant, she saw the young boy with the different colored eyes who used to be her friend. Then the veil descended as Maggie was forced to confront his angry gaze, his pupils dilated with passion and desire.

Just when she thought it might be over, he pulled out and flipped her over. He wrenched her to her knees and entered her again. "This is a good idea," his giggle that of his seven-year-old self. "You're my bitch, so you might as well be swived like one." His erection was as hard and painful as the first time. *How long does it take?* Maggie asked herself. *Will it never end?* There were more ravens now, sounding more desperate and insistent in their calls. Maggie tried to return her mind to the meadow, but with Lyle's every thrust her face was pushed into the grass and dirt, making it harder and harder to breathe. "You're mine," he panted as Maggie felt him pulse inside of her. Lyle groaned with relief, and it was over.

He grabbed her legs and turned her onto her back. She refused to look at him, squeezing her eyes shut. "So, I've left my mark on you, inside and out," he laughed, wheezing from exertion. "No one will question now that you're mine." He grabbed her by the hair and pulled her face to meet his. "Look at me, you whore. Because that's all you are now. You're no good to anyone but me." He kissed her hard, his foul spit smearing beyond her lips. Then he gave her a dainty peck.

He reached and untied the leather straps, then stood over her with his arms outstretched like a victorious warrior. "Remember this day, Maggie, for this is the day you became mine."

"I will never be yours, Lyle," she whispered. With her last bit of strength, she lifted her head and looked into his eyes. "From this day forward, I will hate you forever." Lyle raised the strap above his head to strike her, but stopped when Lennox shouted his name from the top of the hill. He tucked himself into his trousers, ran to his horse, and galloped out of the forest.

The ravens descended from the top of the tree and surrounded her, plucking the leaves from her hair and tearing at the smears of blood on the ground.

Lennox watched Lyle leave, and then glanced to the spot under the tree where the ravens were gathered. Were they feeding on something that had died? His heart stopped when he saw them pecking at Maggie's auburn hair.

Chapter Ten

Lennox raced down the hill, stumbling and slipping in his desperation to get to her. He shooed the ravens away and fell to his knees beside her, devastated by what he saw. "Oh, Mistress. Oh, my Maggie," he murmured, his voice breaking. Her cheeks were swollen and her breasts bruised and bitten, some breaking the skin. His trembling hands pulled her skirts down over her blood-smeared thighs.

Maggie felt hands upon her and moaned in protest, her flailing arms too weak to fight back.

"It's me, Maggie. It's Lennox. You're safe now."

Maggie's eyes opened in horror, her voice barely a whisper. "Don't touch me. Go away…don't touch." She fought to push him away but collapsed as consciousness took its leave. Lennox whistled for Titus and crawled over to where her discarded cloak lay. He closed her shift and corset as best he could, wrapped the cloak around her, and carried her to where Titus stood waiting. He led him to a large boulder, stepped up, and swung into the saddle with Maggie in his arms. He gently urged Titus forward and left the forest to the bickering ravens returning to the spot where Maggie laid.

Lennox held Maggie close, gently kissing her temple and the top of her head through his tears. "I'm sorry, Maggie, I'm sorry." He couldn't say it enough. *I should have been there to protect her. I promised her she'd be safe in the woods. My woods.* He held her to his chest, resting his chin on the top of her head, tears streaming down his cheeks to her auburn hair, soiled by dirt, leaves, and Lyle de Mortimer.

His mind pulled back to the wolf that had loped across his path on the way back from the castle. Titus spooked and fought against the reins in fear, but Lennox calmed him and they continued on, putting the encounter behind them. He blamed himself for not recognizing the sight of the wolf as an omen, a predator always on the hunt for its next victim.

Maggie whimpered and shifted in pain. Lennox adjusted her position and gathered her to him again. "We're almost there, Maggie. Just a wee bit more." He kept to the quiet back street, pulling Titus to a halt at The Weavers Hands. He slid out of the saddle with her in his arms, looking at the parts of her face that hadn't been abused by

Lyle. Her skin was pale and translucent, almost death-like. "Please forgive me, Maggie." He kissed her and entered the back of the shop without knocking.

Angus was preparing a delivery, his back to the door. "Where have you been, lass? I expected you long before now."

"It's me, sir. Lennox Brodie."

Angus turned and clasped his hand to his chest. "God's mercy in Heaven! What happened?"

"She was attacked in the woods – my woods."

Angus frantically cleared the bolts of wool from the worktable. "Lay her down," he said, then hurried to the entrance to the shop. "Graham!" He turned back to Lennox. "My errand boy." He gave Graham a coin and whispered something to him that Lennox couldn't hear - Angus explained when the door closed. "I've sent for the Sorcha, the healer, and told Graham that no one is to know what happened." He clasped Maggie's hand, pained concern on his face. "Do you know who did this?"

"Yes." The answer sounded more like a hiss than an affirmation.

"Then out with it, man! Who is the beast that violated my daughter? Justice must be served somehow."

"I won't reveal his name just yet. You must trust me, sir. Justice will be served, but I mean to do it on my terms. He will pay for what he did to Mistress Maggie, but it will take time for me to put things in place. Until then, please speak of this to no one."

Graham returned with the Sorcha, covered and hooded in a deep, russet cloak. She remained silent, her dark eyes focused on Maggie as she moved immediately to her side. As Lennox was turning to leave, Angus grasped his arm. "Thank you, Sir Brodie, for rescuing my daughter. We will do all that can be done to see her healed." Lennox nodded and closed the door behind him, thankful that no one saw him go weak in the knees and collapse on the ground next to Titus. He struggled into the saddle and clung to the reins, depending on the capable stallion to guide them. "Take us home, Titus."

Titus startled the roosting ravens and brought Lennox out of his emotional fog, igniting his anger like a spark to gunpowder. As he rode through the damp, flattened grass, his eyes locked on the spot where he'd found Maggie. He spurred Titus up the path and galloped him across the clearing before handing him off to Gavin, his groom. He would plan and carry out his revenge on

Lyle de Mortimer, but not tonight. Tonight, anger and guilt would be his loyal drinking companions.

Chapter Eleven

"Goodnight, Darby," Lennox said, taking a bottle of ale from each outstretched hand. "And pay no mind to anything you hear. Cover your ears and leave it be."

"As you say, sir," Darby answered with a look of growing concern on his face. "Goodnight sir."

Lennox didn't bother with a glass. He'd get drunk faster if he swilled it directly from the bottle. He sat in front of the fire, remembering the events of the day - how it began so well and ended so badly. He failed to recognize the omen of the wolf that had crossed his path. He failed to protect Maggie while she was on his lands – something he'd promised her. He failed to keep Lyle de Mortimer away from her. Sir Lennox Brodie, a powerful and honorable knight. Strong and capable. On this day, an utter failure. He threw the empty bottle into the fire and pummeled his fists against the stones until they bled.

He opened the second bottle and drank while he paced around the room. He was relatively certain Maggie would heal from the physical damage inflicted by Lyle, but what about her emotional well-being? She was no longer a virgin - Lyle had seen to that. She would feel the shame of it, of being "soiled goods." What if she blamed herself for what happened? She'd fought against him even though she knew it was him trying to help her. She told him to leave, not to touch her. She tried to push him away. Did Lyle destroy their relationship when he attacked her and took her virginity?

Lennox stopped in front of his two-handed sword and took it down. He held it at arm's length, looking down its dusty surface as his hands tightened on its grip. He drained the bottle, set it on the table, and lopped off the neck with his sword. Lennox marched around the room, bellowing with rage in a combination of languages as he slashed and cut everything within the mighty sword's reach – tables, candlesticks, pottery, and the very chair from which he'd just risen.

The swing of the sword and his hand in the grip transported Lennox back to Jerusalem, back to his battles with the Moors. Fueled by grief, he killed with a vengeance, leaving a swath of death behind him – butchery in the name of victory. Each battle made him thirst for the next. The doomed and desperate fell beneath his sword, his strength and skill in battle fed by his need to make the enemy pay for his own heartbreak and loss.

His name preceded him; it earned him respect and instilled fear in those foolish enough to cross his path. He took women without regard, where and when he wanted, his fame and reputation feeding his lust and sense of entitlement. Sometimes husbands or children would be unwilling witnesses, but Lennox paid them no mind. It didn't take long to get the release he craved.

Out of breath and out of ale, he threw the sword on the hearth and sunk to his knees, ashamed of the man he'd let himself become. Lennox stared into the fire, but what he saw were the faces of the men he'd killed, weeping mothers clutching children to their breasts, and the blank, empty stares of the women he'd violated. Tears of shame and loathing filled his eyes and spilled onto the warm bricks, disappearing as the next took its place. His stomach already convulsing with sobs, he retched and vomited, watching it spill onto his battle-etched sword. He staggered to his feet, opened the door, and ran out into the lightning-streaked night.

Titus nickered when Lennox entered the stable. He stood patiently while Lennox fumbled with the bridle and struggled to pull himself onto his back. They galloped across the windswept meadow in front of the manor house, Lennox ignoring the thunderclaps of the approaching storm. Titus grew uneasy with his drunken signals – pulling on the reins while spurring him forward. He danced sideways and tossed his head, but Lennox clutched his mane and urged him on. "C'mon, my man – let's ride!"

Titus was galloping at full speed when they came to the forest. Lennox chose a path other than the one leading to the glade. The way to the river was steep with sharp turns and low-hanging branches. A flash of lightning frightened Titus. He fought the reins, stumbled, and stopped short, throwing Lennox over his head. He nudged his unconscious master, and then stood waiting patiently, head bowed against the pouring rain.

Chapter Twelve

Maggie was content in her fog-like existence, an imaginary place to dwell between the living and the dead. The potions Sorcha gave her allowed her to float with detached awareness in the world around her - free of pain, fear, and human contact.

She felt the initial sting of her injuries being cleansed and a warm cloth washing her legs and thighs. "Mother?" she moaned, but the only response was a soft shushing and someone telling her it would be alright. Gentle hands brushed her hair and pulled a nightdress over her head. Then, the blessed weight of quilts carried her into a netherworld of neither here nor there, neither life nor death.

She could have stayed there forever if it weren't for the shaft of sunlight that burned through her medicinal haze, jolting her awake. Maggie eased the quilt back and looked for the cup on her bedside table, but it was gone. The door to her room opened, and she dropped back onto the pillow, pulling the quilt tight against her chin. It was Sorcha with a breakfast tray. Her raven-black hair flowed past her waist; her necklaces and bracelets created a metallic, jingling song as she moved into the room. Generations of her family had lived in the stone cottage that hugged the edge of town, surrounded by gardens for food and the medicinal herbs and plants she used in her practice. She was wise and well-respected, living a comfortable, but somewhat eccentric life. The women of Stonehaven were too frightened and suspicious to befriend her, but didn't hesitate to summon her when injury or illness befell a friend or family member. Sorcha set the tray on the bedside table and sat on the bed, taking Maggie's hand in hers.

"Good Morning, Mistress. How are you feeling?"

"I'd feel better with more of whatever it is that you've been giving me."

"Well, that's just it, you see. I think it's time for you to return to the land of the living. Your injuries are just about healed. It's time for you to get out of bed and let the sun shine upon your face. You need to breathe fresh, outside air."

Maggie propped herself against the headboard and took a sip of the warm, honey-sweetened milk. "I may come downstairs after the shop is closed, but I'll not venture out."

"You can't stay behind closed doors for the rest of your life," Sorcha said, her dark eyes meeting Maggie's as she handed her a bannock. "You have to become a part of the world again - you can't let what happened shape who you are. If you do, then whoever did this will have won, and you can't give him that power over you."

Maggie toyed with the quilt, twisting it in her hands.

"What if I'm with child?"

Sorcha looked at her with an uneasy sigh. "There are certain herbs that can be used, but it's too soon to know." Sorcha gently squeezed her hand. "You will let me know if your courses do not come?"

"I will." Maggie managed a quick smile of gratitude at Sorcha's concern.

"Good." Sorcha patted her cheek and rose to leave. "Well, then. Unless you need my help getting dressed, I'll leave you to get yourself out of bed today."

"No, I can manage. Thank you, Sorcha, for all you've done."

"Think nothing of it, lass," she smiled. "Just send word if there's anything you need."

After Sorcha left, Maggie slid back under the quilts and stared at the ceiling. She wished it had been her mother sitting on the bed, counseling her. Sorcha was gentle, kind, and honest, but not her mother – the one who'd taught her to be strong and capable. The one who guided her as she transformed from girl into woman. But her mother was gone these past three years. What advice would she give? Maggie closed her eyes and listened to the voice telling her it was time to face the world again, to move forward with her head held high.

She pushed the quilt aside and pulled herself out of bed. Her abused body ached with the slightest movement, her bruises tender to the touch. She stood in front of the window overlooking the street entrance to the shop, watching people going about their daily lives. Sorcha and her mother were right; she needed to become part of the world again. But how? She knew Lyle was out there somewhere and wouldn't risk encountering him after what had happened.

Lennox groaned in pain as Titus nudged the side of his head and tugged his hair. He was stiff and chilled to the bone, trousers torn, and the gash on his arm oozed blood. He struggled to his feet, leaned against the tree until the world stopped spinning, and hugged Titus for faithfully watching over him. "I'm sorry I was so rough on you last night. Forgive me, boy?" Titus nickered softly and pushed against Lennox's chest. "Seems I'm asking everyone's forgiveness these days. First Maggie, and now you." He took the reins and slowly led Titus up the hill toward home. "If only Maggie's forgiveness would come as swift and complete as yours. I guess there's only one way to find out."

When they reached the stables, Lennox handed Titus off to Gavin. Sturdy and stout, he had a kind, weathered face and dark hair streaked with strands of grey. A man of few words, he preferred to converse with horses rather than people. He looked the knight up and down but said nothing aside from, "I'll see to him, sir."

Lennox mumbled an embarrassed, "thank you" as he began to recall the events of the previous night. The entire household must know by now. He dreaded returning to his quarters and having to face the damage and destruction brought on by his drunken rampage, but his loyal servant Darby had quietly and efficiently worked his magic. The room was clean and restored with replacement furnishings, candlesticks, and the like. His sword, cleaned and oiled, hung in its place near the door, and a crackling fire warmed the room. It was like last night had never happened.

"Thank you, Darby," he said, one hand on each shoulder of the exhausted servant. "I am sorry for all I've put you through."

"Think nothing of it, sir. I'm just glad you're back, and safe. We were right worried when you didn't come home last night." Darby noticed the gash on Lennox's arm, gently lifting his shirt sleeve to inspect it. "You'll want to have Corliss clean and bind that for you – she'll be in the kitchen, fixing you something to eat."

Lennox trudged down the stairs and reluctantly turned the corner leading to the kitchen already humming with activity.

"Hot milk with honey and porridge will put you to rights, as would a sound thrashing," Corliss said as she added two slices of fresh-baked bread to Lennox's breakfast, and then went to work cleansing and bandaging his injured arm. "A hot bath and bed is what you need next."

"I won't argue the bath, but sleep will have to wait until I return from Stonehaven."

"And what's in Stonehaven that demands your immediate attention? Or should I say *who*?"

"An explanation will have to wait, I'm afraid," Lennox said, kissing her on the cheek and putting his finger to his lips, indicating a secret to be kept. "I'm off to my bath and then I'll be on my way."

Darby was waiting at the door with Lennox's cloak and riding gloves. "Thank you, Darby," he said, stepping into the courtyard, then stopped and turned. "Darby, would you please find the maps of my land holdings and leave them on the table in my room?" He laughed when he saw the look of concern on Darby's face. "I assure you I won't destroy them."

"Very well, sir. I shall see to it right away."

"Thank you, Darby. Oh, one more thing."

"Yes sir?"

"After you've done that, take a nap – you look positively exhausted."

"As you wish, sir," Darby answered with a nod and a weary smile.

Mindful that Titus was just as tired as he, Lennox let him set the pace across the clearing, past the grave, and down the path into the glade. His body tensed as they grew closer and stiffened in alarm when they startled a doe standing in the spot where Lyle had attacked Maggie. The doe bounded off with her tail raised in alarm, causing Titus to halt with a snort. He calmed when Lennox patted his neck and reassured him, and they continued out of the forest onto the road that led to Stonehaven and The Weavers Hands.

Chapter Thirteen

Beneath the window, a whinny pulled Maggie's attention to the horse tied in front of the shop. It was Titus, Lennox's stallion. She backed away from the window, the gasp of alarm sharp and painful in her chest. She couldn't face him and knew he would never venture to her room, even if it was something as honorable as asking after her welfare. Still, she hurried to the door and slid the lock into place. As she leaned against it, she heard him conversing with her father downstairs, their voices floating to her through the slotted opening in the floor next to her wardrobe.

She grimaced in pain as lowered herself to peer through the opening. Lennox stood with his back to her line of sight. She silently admired his black, wavy hair, woolen cloak, and freshly-shined boots. His physical presence and mannerisms captivated her; his gestures, the twist of his head that showed her the scar on his cheek, and his strong, capable hands. Maggie's heart warmed at the sight of him, but her smile vanished when she thought about what he'd seen when he discovered her in the woods. Much of their conversation was in hushed tones, but the words "healing" and "see her" reached her ears.

Maggie mouthed the word 'no' and shook her head. The shame of what Lyle had done to her was too raw and painful for her to consider the possibility of coming face-to-face with Lennox. Her heart ached with sorrow for the only man she'd ever loved. He would never accept her after what had happened, her fault or not. Her virginity was gone. She was 'soiled goods', a whore – that's what Lyle called her. The entire town would have heard about it by now, with Lyle's bragging. Had her father learned it was Lyle who attacked her? If he had, he'd be wanting a conversation with her about it soon enough. Tears filled her eyes and dropped through the opening in the floor as Lennox said goodbye to her father and closed the door behind him. She crawled back to bed and sobbed under the quilts, mourning her dreams of a life that might have been.

It was late afternoon when Maggie heard someone push against the lock, then knock. "Who is it?" she asked, jumping up and holding her hand against the hasp.

"It's me, Maggie – open the door. I'd like a word." She stepped aside to admit her father and closed the door behind them. She sat on the edge of the bed; he pulled up a chair to face her and took her hands in his. "I'm sorry for what happened to you – truly, I am. And, I know who did it, but we'll not speak of that just now. I entrusted Sorcha with your care and took her advice about giving you time to heal. She told me this morning that you're well enough to come down and help again in the shop."

"How can I show my face when everyone that comes in will know?" She pulled her hands from his and walked to the window. "What if Lyle comes into the shop? What then?"

Angus stood and joined her at the window. "You conduct yourself in the shop as if none of this ever happened. If Lyle comes in, go to the back room at once and stay with the other workers until he is removed." He gently hugged her and kissed her forehead. "I'm nearly out of dye materials, so tomorrow you can go gathering on Stuart Campbell's lands if you'd rather not venture onto the Lennox property."

"I don't want to go anywhere alone."

"Aye, I've thought of that. I'll send Graham with you. He'll bring Duffy, of course – he's a good watchdog. You'll be fine, Maggie. Besides, I've gotten word that Lyle left for Perth yesterday and won't be back for several weeks. That may help put your mind at ease." He leaned in and gently kissed her cheek. "It will work itself out, Maggie."

After he left, Maggie went to the bedside table and opened her book to the page that held the pressed rose Lennox had given her the day they'd shared lunch in the glade. Its scent was faint, the papery petals transparent in the soft, afternoon light. The rose was a symbol of love and devotion – a token Lennox had given her before Lyle attacked and raped her. He could never love her now. She would have to be content with the memory and the dream that could never come true.

Lennox moved his supper dishes to the table by the door and spread out the maps Darby delivered earlier in the day. After careful study, he marked a dozen plots that he no longer needed and drafted a plan for gifting them. It was an unusual gesture. Landowners rarely disposed of lands they held, let alone give them away. Lennox's land holdings were extensive and gifting the parcels would help those less fortunate in life. He would set aside a special day, post notices throughout Stonehaven and the castle, and make it a day like a festival, complete with feasting and entertainment. It would be held in the meadow in front of his new manor house.

He sat with quill and paper, working late into the night. No ale passed his lips in the minutes and hours that followed; he needed his wits about him, for this was more than gifting land and providing food and entertainment. What happened on this day would determine the course of the rest of his life.

Chapter Fourteen

Graham was waiting at the back entrance to The
Weavers Hands with Duffy, his fawn-colored deerhound.
Graham was fifteen and growing as fast as a willow. His
rosy-brown curls and dark blue eyes were already catching
the attention of the young lasses in Stonehaven. But
Graham was a polite, well-mannered young man not yet
ready for female attachments. His parents had seen to that,
keeping him busy at the mill and at church on Sundays.
"Good Morning, Mistress. Where would you like to go this
morning?"

"Good Morning, Graham." Maggie stroked Duffy's
wiry coat and pulled the door shut behind her. She looked
around with apprehension, and then gave Graham the
bravest smile she could muster. "Thank you for coming
with me today. Let's go to the Campbell lands. I haven't
been there in some time, and I think I remember where I
can get what I need."

The path leading to the Campbell lands was north of
those belonging to Lennox, and Maggie was grateful for
that. She couldn't bear to venture near the spot where Lyle

had attacked and raped her. Her father assured her that Lyle was away, but Maggie had no idea where Lennox was and didn't want to risk having to face him after what had happened and what he'd seen.

The fresh, summer air lifted Maggie's spirits. Sorcha was right. She needed to feel the sun on her skin - nature would help her heal. She gathered a few things along the way - those that needed full sun to flourish and bloom. Graham let Duffy off his lead; he bounded around them in circles, then stopped, alert to any movement that required his attention.

The small group strolled into the shade of the forest. Maggie told Graham about the various plants and their uses as he walked alongside her. He told her about his family and the new brother or sister that would be arriving before summer's end. Maggie's chest tightened, but she forced herself to smile and ask Graham what he was hoping for. Her courses had not come, but it was too early for her to be concerned.

Maggie pushed the thought from her mind and continued on with her tasks. After an hour, she had almost everything she needed. Her basket was nearly full as she followed Graham up a long foothill she had never taken.

Duffy ran ahead at intervals and then waited for them to catch up.

Maggie gathered the rock lichen and blaeberry her father needed and met Graham at the top of the hill. Her breath caught in her throat; nothing could have prepared her for what lay before them.

The abbey ruin looked as though it was in the midst of a transformation, of becoming part of the forest. Birds flew in and out of the window openings and perched on the vines crawling up its mossy, stone walls. Saplings muscled their way between the paving stones leading to the entrance hall. Pieces of the structure lay toppled, brought down by time, storms, and neglect. What remained standing were jagged spires held aloft by the sturdy foundation walls that continued to resist nature's efforts to reclaim them.

Graham told Maggie he had a bit of 'personal business' to attend to and would wait for her at the entrance when he was finished. Maggie left her basket at the doorway, telling Graham she wouldn't be long; she just wanted a quick look inside.

She stepped into the once-regal hall, now a crumbling, forgotten place of kings, knights, and maidens. Scenic tapestries hung in tatters, their colorful, woven stories faded into brittle paragraphs. Voices of chanting monks floated on the dusty air, their rhythmic echoes rising with the swirling columns trying to find a way to Heaven.

The broken windows underfoot felt like the pieces of her own shattered heart, their fragile bits confirming what she already felt to be true. "He'll never love you now," one laughed. "Soiled goods," hissed another. She picked her way carefully among them. "Romantic fool." Maggie didn't have the strength or will to answer them. They were right, after all.

She hummed silently with the monks as she moved away from the cruel, broken glass and sat on the cold, empty steps that once led to the throne of the king. She stroked the smooth, grey stone. How many men knelt in this very spot, waiting for the touch of the sword on their shoulders, transforming them from man to knight?

Lennox had been bestowed this great honor. She imagined how handsome he must have looked with his sword and shield, taking his oath in the adoubement ceremony. He would have worn a white vesture, covered by a red robe. Head bowed and kneeling, his shoulders would have felt the sword as he swore his oath of allegiance.

The waves of sadness returned as they had countless times since the attack in the forest. Tears welled up and spilled onto the stones - dark drops of sorrow and remembrance for a love and a life that would never be. Maggie muffled her sobs so Graham would not hear, but she could hear him talking to Duffy.

Then her head snapped up in alarm. There were two male voices, not one. She swiped at her eyes, stood, and looked for a place to hide until she could determine who was talking to Graham. She turned into an alcove and stopped short. Lennox stepped out of the shadows and greeted her with a bow.

"Are you well, Mistress Maggie? Are you quite healed from your injuries?" Panicked and embarrassed, Maggie backed away and tried to go around him, but he raised his hand, asking her to stop. "I called on your father several times, asking after your welfare, but he didn't think it fitting that I should see you."

"I'm quite well, so you needn't bother inquiring again," she said, her voice breaking. "Please, Lennox, please let me pass. Graham will be wondering..."

"Not until you hear me out. I've already spoken to Graham. He will wait outside for us." The sun came out from behind a cloud and streamed through an empty window, lighting the alcove where they stood, face-to-face. "What happened in the glade…"

"Please, I'm so ashamed. Can't you see?"

"Maggie, what happened was not your fault! Lyle forced himself upon you. There's no shame in that. The shame is mine – those are my lands. I promised to protect you, and I failed." He slowly stepped closer to her. "Maggie, do you not know that I've loved you from moment I first laid eyes on you?" He raised his right hand and gently let his finger trace along her cheekbone, bringing it to rest under her chin.

His dark eyes were intent upon hers, searching their depths and exploring the rest of her face. "Why are you looking at me like that?" she asked.

Lennox laughed softly. "I've traveled the world over and seen a great many women, but none compare to the beauty that stands before me in this ruined, crumbling abbey." The clear-eyed smile she returned warmed his heart and healed a small part of his soul. He opened his arms to her, and she stepped in. Gently he enfolded her, doing his best to replace some of the pain and abuse she'd suffered at Lyle's hands. "Oh, Maggie, I do love you," he sighed with pleasure. "And nothing will ever change that."

"Are you sure?"

"As sure as I've been of anything in my life." He softly touched her bottom lip with his thumb. He looked from her lips to her eyes. "May I kiss you, Maggie? I promise to be gentle."

She looked up at him, tears filling her eyes, and Lennox stepped back.

"I'm sorry, Maggie. I never meant to upset you."

"You didn't." She took both of his hands in hers. "I never thought this day would happen, so it's a bit overwhelming."

"Then I may?"

Maggie smiled, tilting her head to meet his eyes. "Of course you may."

Lennox placed his hands on either side of her neck and gently kissed her lips. He remembered their softness, the way they fit perfectly with his. Desire surged through his body, but he held himself back, ignoring what his hormones ordered him to do. It was difficult because Maggie returned his kisses willingly, responding to the movement of his lips on hers. He knew she was still fragile, still recovering, and he needed to be mindful and restrain himself. And yet…

"Mistress Maggie?" Graham's voice echoed through the vast, empty hall. His voice cut into the safe, warm world she and Lennox had just entered. Maggie stepped back, her face flushed as she smoothed her gown and adjusted her cloak.

"Yes, Graham, what is it?"

"Mistress, looks like rain coming. We should be making our way back."

"I'll be right there." She smiled at Lennox. "I must go."

Lennox walked her out of the abbey hall, resting his hand on her back. He felt the need to protect her and wanted to touch her until they reached the entrance. "When can I see you again?"

"I don't know," she whispered. "Father wants me to accompany him to Market Day on Saturday. If you were to attend, we can speak there."

"I want to do more than speak," he whispered back.

Chapter Fifteen

For the first time in her life, Maggie looked forward to Market Day at Castle Wrought, for it brought with it the hope of seeing Lennox. Her lips remembered his kiss, and the warm security of his embrace surrounded her like a warm, safe blanket.

The atmosphere on the clear, July afternoon seemed more confusing, congested, and chaotic than she remembered. People and animals were getting tangled up with one another and tempers flared. A bull pulled away from its owner and pursued a cow in season. That started a chain reaction of scattered geese, pigs, and sheep. Carts collided with one another and more than one overturned, scattering a mix of carrots, pottery, and metalwork on the ground.

Maggie watched from behind their table, thankful to be away from the confusion with her father was standing next to her. Some passersby watched her with knowing stares. Some snickered while others gave her quick, sympathetic smiles. Maggie concentrated on their customers as she wrapped purchases and made change. She glanced up now and then, looking for Lennox; a small stab of disappointment tapped at her heart when her eyes did not find his.

"I'll be but a minute, Maggie," her father said, stepping away from behind their stall. Maggie felt uneasy at his leaving. "I can smell that boar roasting – I'll bring us back a bite to eat."

"Alright, but please hurry back."

Maggie watched her father leave and then scanned the crowd for Lennox's tall stature, dark hair, and eyes. Then something changed. Without meaning or conscious thought, her eyes gravitated toward the shoppers with copper-colored hair. Her mind sought reassurance that Lyle had indeed gone to Perth, but what should have been reassurance turned to fear. Her hands trembled and grew damp with sweat, yet felt numb as they would have in winter. She scanned the crowd with more intensity, breathing faster and feeling her heart race in her chest. Then her eyes locked on the man standing across the walkway from her. He looked like Lyle, had the same copper-colored hair, but it wasn't him. It was his brother, Wilfred.

He leaned against a post, smiling at her. Then his lips formed a kiss and his tongue wagged in a lecherous, disgusting way. His right hand traveled down to his crotch as Maggie watched in horror while he cupped and fondled himself. Then he stepped forward and brushed his hands together as one would when finished with a task.

He approached Maggie and leaned over the table. She stepped back in disgust at the smell and the fleas jumping from the filthy shirt covered in what looked like strands of sheep's wool.

"Remember me, Maggie? I'm Lyle's younger brother, Wilfred. Here to welcome you into the family, so to speak."

"I have no idea what you're talking about. Please go away and leave me alone."

Wilfred leaned closer, forcing Maggie to cover her nose to keep from gagging. His eyes were blue, unlike Lyle's one blue and one green. Still, the resemblance was unmistakable. His mouth moved, but all Maggie could focus on was the glob of dried snot trapped in his mangy beard, the pimples that peppered his forehead, and the one on his nose that looked like it was about to burst. When he smiled, the canals of dried food at the corners of his mouth cracked and flaked off like dried, diseased skin.

"Well, we're a right close family - we share and share alike. And since Lyle's away at Perth, I think it's time I got my share. See, he told me all about your little meeting in the woods."

Maggie's eyes widened in fright and disbelief. Her chest tightened as she struggled to breathe, and white spots flickered behind her eyes.

"We can meet in the same place, or I can collect you from your little shop." When he licked his lips, a thread of saliva oozed out and dripped off the end of his tongue. "No need to bathe, I'll take you quick and deep, just like…"

Wilfred never saw the fist coming before it connected with his jaw. He staggered back, landing in the middle of the walkway. Onlookers shrieked and backed away, creating a space for Lennox to grab hold and haul him to his feet. Blood oozed from his nose and mouth as Wilfred coughed and choked, gasping for air. Lennox remained silent, his anger well past any rational thought or desire for words.

The cobbled walkway echoed Lennox's striding steps and Wilfred's stumbling, tripping attempts to remain upright. With the ease of tossing a stone into a river, Lennox swung Wilfred past him, releasing him to tumble down the stone steps leading to the stables. Wilfred landed motionless at the bottom, a slow trickle of blood from his head confirming his demise.

Assured of Wilfred's death, Lennox ran back to reassure Maggie, but she was gone. Angus was leaning over behind their stall, away from the curious onlookers.

"What's happened, Angus?"

"I don't know. When I heard the ruckus, I hurried back. This is how I found her."

Maggie was on the grass, curled in a ball, with her hands over her face. She shook like a leaf, her muffled sobs drowned out by the rumble of thunder. Angus looked from her to the piles of woolen fabric and other goods strewn about in his stall. "I need to load up before the storm hits. Can you help me with her, Lennox?"

"Aye, I'll see that's she's brought somewhere safe and looked after. Don't worry yourself if she's not back until morning. No harm will come to her, I assure you." A strong gust flapped the stall curtains as Angus wrung his hands, flustered with indecision and anxious to fill his cart and be on his way.

Lennox lifted Maggie in his arms, gathering her cloak around her. "I'll see her safe, Angus." He took the back way to the stables, found Titus, and crossed the courtyard as the first raindrops fell.

Chapter Sixteen

Maggie jerked to awareness in Lennox's arms. She fought against him, unsure of where she was or who was holding her.

"Shh... it's me, Maggie. Lennox. You're safe now. Just rest against me and close your eyes." He pulled her cloak tight against the rain and pulled his own over her, sheltering her as best he could. She quieted and pressed against his chest. He knew just where to go - the empty farmer's cottage on his property was safe, quiet, and private. No one would come looking for them there.

He guided Titus to the lean-to and slid from the saddle with Maggie in his arms. He'd tend to him later; at least he was secure and out of the rain. He grabbed his saddle bag and shut the gate behind him.

"Where are we?" Maggie asked, cringing with the next bolt of lightning.

"Just a wee cottage on my property. It's quiet here and no one will disturb us." He hurried through the rain toward the rough-hewn building snugged against a hill that watched over a quiet, slow-moving stream.

Lennox set Maggie down and closed the door. She was shivering from the cold, her rain-soaked cloak, and the trauma she'd suffered as a result of Wilfred's unwelcome advances. Lennox guided her to a chair next to the fireplace.

"You sit here while I light a fire." He pulled a patchwork quilt from the rustic, four-poster bed and held it out to her. "You'll want to take off that wet cloak."

"Thank you," she said, exchanging one for the other. Lennox hung it on a peg and set himself to the task of fire-building. He knelt in front of the dark, rough-stoned fireplace, his hands shaking as he lit the tinder and added small bits of wood. He hadn't given himself time to react to the encounter and subsequent death of Wilfred, the feeling of helplessness at not showing up sooner so that he could have intercepted Maggie's subjection to his lewd behavior, and the excitement and uncertainty of being alone with her.

The blazing fire took the chill from the small room as Lennox removed his own cloak and hung it next to hers. He set his saddle bag on the table and removed a bottle of ale and some bread and cheese wrapped in a cloth. He pulled up a stool next to her, offering her the meager bits he had. "I'm sorry it's not more…"

"Please – how could you have known this would happen?" She smiled, took a sip of ale, and handed the bottle back to him. "Thank you. I'll be fine, really. It just takes a bit of time to recover."

"Well, we won't be going anywhere until the storm passes. Not until morning." He watched her face for a reaction to the fact that she'd be spending the night alone with him.

Maggie looked at him in alarm. "My father – he'll wonder where I am."

Lennox took her hand and kissed it. "He knows you're with me, Maggie. He knows no harm will come to you."

Lennox banked the fire as the evening wore on. They relaxed in its warmth and the peaceful intimacy of being alone together. He watched Maggie gradually recover from the incident with Wilfred, but his name would not be spoken tonight. He studied her face as she started telling him a story, mesmerized by her beauty and the way her eyes sparkled in the firelight.

"I had this dream," Maggie laughed. "I was a wee girl and met a boy my own age, maybe a bit older. We were sweethearts, I guess. We were sitting on a riverbank on a

summer afternoon. We shared an innocent kiss, promised
our hearts to each other, and swore a pact that we'd marry
when we came of age."

"When did you last have this dream?"

"Oh, I don't know. It's been years. Why?"

"You're not going to believe this," Lennox
answered. "I've had the same dream. The last time was
when I was in Jerusalem, of all places. I don't know why,
or what brought it on, but there it is."
Maggie held out her arms. "It gives me gooseflesh to hear
it. How can that be?"

"I don't know how the world works, Maggie, but
it's God's honest truth."

Lennox reluctantly stood and donned his cloak. "I
need to tend to Titus – he's still saddled, and I need to
make sure he has hay and water. I won't be long."

Maggie stood with him. "I need to step outside as
well. You know. To, um…" She laughed nervously, her
cheeks flushing from more than the heat of the fireplace.

Lennox smiled. "Please, I understand. I will be
tending to Titus, so you will know where I am. You can
choose a private spot that suits you."

Taking care of Titus gave Lennox time to think and a chance to try and calm his nerves. He felt like a young school boy with a childhood crush, but Maggie was no school girl, and he was a full-grown man. She wasn't someone whose purpose it was to merely to satisfy an urge, a lustful need. He'd done that plenty of times in the past. Oh, he wanted her, but he also loved her, and that made all the difference in the world.

He knew what he wanted to happen when he went back inside. Did she want the same? She'd endured more than her fair share of trauma at Lyle's hands, and he didn't want to be the cause of additional pain, emotional or otherwise. His physical urges were telling him one thing, his conscience another. Perhaps a compromise could be reached. He prayed for one as he gathered an armload of wood.

Maggie was standing in front of the fire when he returned. He emptied the wood into the box next to the hearth, only to jump back in alarm, cursing under his breath.

"What is it?" Maggie asked.

"A spider."

"I could have guessed," she laughed. She seemed relaxed and at ease knowing they'd be spending the night together alone. It wasn't just the ale. She took several swallows and handed him the bottle. "I think I've reached my limit."

He took a significant mouthful and set the bottle on the table. His heart was pounding in his chest, his palms sweating as he moved across the room to where Maggie stood. He faced her, his dark eyes looking down into hers. "May I touch you?"

"Yes," she breathed.

Chapter Seventeen

He began with her hair, gently untying the saffron ribbon that bound it, releasing the waves of auburn that fell to her shoulders and beyond. He gathered a lock and held it to his face, breathing in the scent of lavender and spice. She lowered her head, leaving Lennox unsure of what she was feeling.

He put his finger under her chin and gently raised it. Her eyes were trusting, yet fearful, begging him to be gentle and careful with her. He traced his finger across her bottom lip, feeling her breathe in and out, pleased by his touch. He brought his hands to her face and cradled it, kissing her softly at first, then more deeply. She pulled away at the touch of his tongue, covering her mouth with her hand. "I'm sorry," she said. Tears filled her eyes as she tried to explain. "It's just that…"

"It's okay, Maggie. I'll be gentle." He tenderly kissed away her tears and held her to his chest, his strong, powerful arms forming a safe embrace. Maggie pressed herself against him, listening to the steady, secure rhythm of his heart. He stood there, patient and silent, holding her until she felt safe again. Then she stepped back, looked up at him, and put her hands around his waist.

"Can we try again?" he asked. When she nodded, he lowered his head and placed his lips upon hers, feeling how perfectly matched they were, elated by her open, welcoming response.

Maggie stepped away and turned her back to him, pulled on the laces to loosen her dark, emerald dress, inviting him to finish. As she turned to face him, it slipped it from her shoulders and slid to the floor around her feet. "More laces," she laughed nervously, looking down at her softly-patterned corset.

Lennox kissed her again, long and slow, to put her at ease. Stepping back, he loosened his linen shirt and pulled it off over his head. Maggie stared at his well-muscled chest, covered in a forest of jet-black hair. She sighed openly, then smiled up at him. "I don't know the exact words, but you are well made." She touched his chest with the palms of her hands, circled out to run her hands over his shoulders and down his arms. When they returned to his chest, she kissed its very center.

Lennox untied the bow of her corset, ignoring the insistent demands of his raging hormones. He was

determined to make this first love-making with Maggie
something she'd remember without fear or pain – at least as
painless as he could make it. He placed a finger in the
crossing of each lace, gently and slowly pulling them free.
He tossed it aside, leaving Maggie clad in nothing but her
thin, white shift.

He felt his mouth open as a long rush of air filled
his lungs, then escaped back into the room. His eyes
traveled from hers to the form barely concealed - her erect
nipples, the curve of her waist and hips, and the russet hair
nestled between her legs. It took all the restraint Lennox
possessed not to carry her to the bed and take her right then
and there.

He took her hands and kissed each finger, giving
each its own turn before pressing them back against his
chest. The sound of her breathing reassured Lennox that
Maggie was at ease and enjoying the attention he was
giving her. Still, he wanted to be sure. "Are you alright?"
he whispered in her ear. Her immediate nod and kisses in
response set him in motion. He pulled her to him, kissing
her forehead, her cheeks, and then her mouth. In one
smooth motion, he gathered her into his arms, his lips still
on hers and her arms wrapped around his neck.

He set her down next to the bed with her back to him, knowing she'd be more at ease with his gradual discovery of her naked body. He eased the shift from her shoulders, letting his hands follow it to her waist before letting it go. His height gave him the advantage of looking over her shoulder as his hands caressed her soft, firm breasts, white as the first snowdrops of spring. Her hand covered his in acceptance and pleasure as she turned her head, seeking the reassurance of his lips on hers.

Now it was Lennox's turn to be nervous as he stepped out of his trousers. He felt Maggie's eyes on him even though she turned away as he looked at her, embarrassed, but smiling. "You and Titus could be brothers." Lennox laughed, caught off guard by her observation. Without the constriction of fabric, restraint would be nearly impossible. Lennox groaned, uncertain how much longer he could wait. He'd never had to practice this kind of self-discipline.

Maggie took his hands, kissed them, and guided them to her breasts. Arching her back, she lifted her face to his, seeking his lips. Lennox kissed her thoroughly, traveling to her neck, breasts, and then her lips again. She responded to his gentle, instinctive touch with a breathy moan in his ear as he led her to the bed and laid her on the woolen blanket.

He held himself over her and felt her knees relax and open to him. He entered her slowly - as slowly as he could. He'd been having his own, private battle with arousal since he first laid eyes on her and was eager to breach her private chamber. Maggie inhaled through her teeth. "I'm sorry," he whispered. "Should I stop?" She shook her head as his mouth covered hers and his arms wrapped around her, holding her close. Within seconds they moved as one. She responded to his touch and guidance, trusting him and answering with her hands, lips, and legs that wrapped around him at the last. Unable to hold back any longer, his final thrust spilled himself into her. "Oh Maggie!" he moaned, collapsing on her, fully spent and utterly satisfied.

Maggie kissed his damp, trembling shoulder and held him to her. She couldn't have foreseen what had just happened between them when she'd set out with her father for Market Day. What she'd experienced was so unlike what Lyle had done to her. Yes, there'd been pain at first but, then pleasure and enjoyment. She loved the idea of this strong, powerful man naked and somewhat vulnerable in her arms. She'd given herself to him because she loved him, and nothing in the world outside the four walls of the small cottage would ever change what she felt for him. She closed her eyes and drifted off to sleep, the rhythm of her breathing matching his.

He took her again, fiercely, in the darkest depth of night and again, gently and tenderly, as the first light of dawn crept into the eastern sky.

Chapter Eighteen

Maggie grimaced and then smiled as Lennox lifted her into the saddle.

"I've got sore bits of my own," he laughed, wincing as he swung up behind her. "I think a warm bath is in order - pity we can't take one together."

"Perhaps we need some time apart to rest and heal," she said, wrapping her arms around him and tugging on his beard. He responded with a deep, thorough kiss.

"Let's make a plan going forward," he said as he nudged Titus. "You won't gather in the woods alone, at least not until I can be assured of your safety. If Graham is not available, then send word and I or one of my men will accompany you. I won't risk Lyle getting near you again."

"Thank you," she answered, barely a whisper. The warmth of the sun, the motion of Titus' walk, and Lennox's powerful, solid body holding her lulled her to sleep. Lennox kissed her forehead and sighed deeply, pulling her tighter to his chest.

"I love you, Maggie."

She woke when Titus stopped at the back entrance to The Weavers Hands. Lennox helped her down as Angus opened the door.

"Are you alright, lass?" he asked, relieved to see her safely home. "You'd best come inside."

"I'm fine, father. Just a bit tired, that's all."

Lennox kissed Maggie's hand in farewell as she stepped inside, turned and smiled, finally slipping from view. "I won't stay," he told Angus. "I have matters to attend to." He told Angus of the plan to ensure Maggie's safety on her gathering trips, then mounted Titus and returned home.

He handed Titus off to Gavin and asked Darby to prepare a hot bath. While he waited, he listed the information that would appear on the notices he'd distribute announcing his land-gifting. He'd take it to the printer tomorrow.

Lennox slipped into the hot water with a sigh of relief. The warmth soothed his body and the parts of him that hadn't been active for a very long time. He smiled as he thought about Maggie and how he loved everything about her. It warmed his heart as he recalled how she'd opened up to him, emotionally and physically. He closed his eyes, remembering the smell of Maggie's hair, the touch of her skin, and the sound of her laughter. He smiled as he imagined their lives moving forward together.

He was drifting off when a stomping noise, like those of heavy boots, brought him to high alert. He sat up and looked around, but there was no one in the room and no one at the door. Just as he settled back, his sword slipped from is sheath and fell to the floor. Its tip pierced the wooden floorboard, and the wavering weapon caught the light of the sun, sending shafts of light streaking around the entire room. When the sword slowed and finally stopped, the light shone directly into Lennox's eyes. He shielded it with his hand and let his mind accept what he had just been shown.

He stepped out of the tub, reached for a cloth, and looked out the window as he rubbed himself dry. The blooms of the yellow besom reminded him of the ribbon that he'd untied from Maggie's hair; he smiled when he thought about it and everything that had transpired afterwards.

A movement outside the window caught his attention as he pulled on his trousers. It was a male dog pursuing a female. She was probably in season, he thought, but perhaps not yet ready to mate. The persistent and larger male bit and pulled at the female, who responded with yips and cries of pain. Gavin ran out of the stable to rescue her, but the scene lowered a curtain of rage over Lennox's face. His eyes darkened in anger, his jaw tightened, and his mind returned him to the scene of Lyle de Mortimer standing over his raped and bloodied Maggie. He howled with fury, cursing in a foreign language, clearing the surface of his desk with one thrust of his powerful, muscular arm. He wanted blood, and he wanted it to be Lyle's.

Fists clenched, he stood over the clutter, struggling to re-gain control of his emotions. Next to the scattered papers, he noticed the wee bluebell that Maggie had given him when they left the cottage. His heart calmed as he plucked it from the scattered mess, held it to his nose, and then placed it inside the cover of his Gaelic poetry book. He reassured a startled Darby that all was well and quietly restored order to the room.

Fresh from her bath, Maggie slipped a clean gown over her head and brushed the tangles from her hair. She smiled at the reason for its unruliness - Lennox's hands grasping it while kissing her and their passionate lovemaking under the quilt throughout the night.

She sat next to the window and stared at the distant forests and peaks of mountains beyond the borders of the town. Somewhere out there, Lennox had fought countless battles as a knight, taking the lives of others to fulfill his sworn duty. He'd led a life of violence, and some of that had returned home with him. Her father had told her about Wilfred's swift and violent death at the hands of Lennox. She'd pushed the encounter with him to a dark corner of her mind. Lennox hadn't mentioned it to her when they'd reached the cottage, and she was glad for it. She didn't want Wilfred's unpleasant advances to intrude upon their time alone.

Lennox had been polite and attentive, passionate and gentle. Every bit of him strong, masculine, and full of desire. In the quiet moments after his release, he'd listened, laughed, and shared small parts of himself that she doubted anyone else knew. Like his inability to sleep without a lit candle in the room. The dark brought the demons and the dreams where he heard the crying of a child, but when the child turned around, it was he. He was the wee boy crying - lost, alone, and frightened. She remained silent as he talked, kissing his hand and holding it to her in silent affirmation. She had met the knight. Now she was coming to know the man beneath the armor.

She saw nothing of the haunted ferocity that she'd heard others speak of when describing him. Still, she knew it existed. Wilfred's death was proof of it. Perhaps with time he could face his demons and put them to rest. Perhaps they could heal each other.

Her thoughts were interrupted by a knock at the door. She reluctantly left her thoughts of Lennox and opened the door. It was Sorcha. "Good Afternoon, Maggie. I was passing by and wanted to inquire after your well-being. How are you feeling?"

"Much better, thank you."

Sorcha followed Maggie into the room, her personal scent a mix of herbs and oils. She took the chair opposite Maggie's at the window. "Your father told me about the incident with Wilfred at Market Day. Are you quite recovered?"

"Yes, I'm fine." She stood and moved away from the window, not wanting to reveal what had happened between her and Lennox.

"And, your courses? Have they come?"

"Not yet, but they're only a bit late. It's happened before."

"Sometimes trauma can upset the cycle, so perhaps no need for concern just yet."

"No, not at all."

Sorcha rose to leave, giving Maggie's hand a squeeze. "If you need me, just send word."

"I will. Thank you, Sorcha, for your concern and your visit."

Sorcha closed the door behind her, leaving Maggie to think about their conversation as she watched the people in the street below. A heavily pregnant woman stopped and greeted her friend holding an infant in her arms. They chatted happily, the pregnant woman cradling her bulging belly with her hands as the other offered what looked like words of reassurance.

"Surely that won't be me," Maggie whispered as she turned away.

Chapter Nineteen

Lennox lifted Maggie into the saddle and sat behind her, holding her respectfully close as curious onlookers watched them leave The Weavers Hands. He felt her body tense and heard her breath quicken when they reached the entrance to the glade. He held her close and kissed her cheek. "I'm here, Maggie. No harm will come to you."

"I know, and thank you. It's just that it's the first time I've been back here since…" It was true, but it was also a convenient mask for her concern surrounding her late courses without having to tell Lennox. She wouldn't tell him until she was sure.

"I understand. Perhaps we'll start by the river." He left Titus in the center of the glade to graze. He was as good as a watchdog and would alert Lennox if anyone ventured near.

When they reached the river, Lennox watched the tension fall away from Maggie as if she were removing a garment. In silence he turned, put his hands on each side of her face, and kissed her deeply and passionately. "I've missed you, Maggie," he breathed, holding her close. "I don't like being apart from you."

"Nor I." They walked hand in hand, stopping now and again to pick what she needed. Lennox remained alert without alarming Maggie, pretending to take in the surroundings. He felt uneasy in this peaceful, quiet setting. The battlefield and the immediacy of combat was where he felt most at home. He was in command there; he knew what was expected of him and what had to be done. In this beautiful space he felt powerless, as if the world were closing in on him.

"Can we sit for a moment?" he asked her.

They found a broad, flat boulder and sat next to each other, watching the river and the eider ducks feeding in a quiet pool. "What is it? You seem unsettled today," Maggie said, taking his hand. "What's troubling you?"

"I don't know how to tell you," he said kissing her hand, then studying it. "You'll think me weak, less of a man."

"Nonsense." She turned his head so that his eyes met hers. "Do you not trust me with your feelings after all we've shared?"

"That bird – do you hear its cry? It sounds like a man, screaming in pain. The wind in the trees sound like clashing swords. I am not on the battlefield, but I can't escape what I've seen and done. Places like this, where it's tranquil and still, give the demons a place to torture me." His eyes filled with tears, and his body trembled. He curled over in pain and sobbed. "I swore an oath to God and my king. I fulfilled my duty to my king, and God took my wife and children." Maggie covered Lennox with her cloak, held him close, and gently stroked his back. "How can I go anywhere but Hell after what I've done?"

Maggie knelt down in front of Lennox, took his hands in hers, and looked into his eyes. "You swore an oath, and you upheld it. God will know you are a man of your word. And your wife and daughters died of sickness, of famine, not because of anything you did or didn't do. Can you try to see that?" She reached up and wiped the tears from his cheeks, kissing each one in turn. "I love you, Lennox," she whispered. "Nothing can change that."

Lennox gave her a brief smile and kissed her. "Is it weak to need a woman as much as I need you?"

"No, I think that's love," she said as he pulled her to him. He started to say something but was interrupted by

Titus' anxious whinny. His demeanor shifted in a heartbeat. He masked his vulnerability as took Maggie's hand and strode toward Titus and the glade.

Astride his chestnut mare, Lyle de Mortimer stared at the spot where he'd attacked Maggie with a satisfied grin on his face. Titus was tense but calmed when Lennox took the reins and patted his neck. Lennox stood with one arm outstretched with Maggie behind it. She could feel the heat of his anger, the smell of him wanting to kill Lyle.

She forced herself to breathe slowly and not betray the tightness in her chest and fearful, pounding heart. It would be just the thing to please Lyle and spur Lennox to some action he might come to regret.

"You have reason to venture onto my lands – tell me."

"Good Afternoon, Sir Lennox Brodie. And you, Mistress Maggie." He said her name with a knowing smile and a wink. Maggie refused to react, held her head high, and took a step closer to Lennox's outstretched arm. "I think there is a matter of the ownership of these lands, you see. My father worked for yours, and he told me he was given these lands in a deathbed promise."

"You've no proof other than a dying man's coveting," Lennox responded in an even, menacing tone.

"Well, we can dispute that later. My visit today is in reference to the notice for the land-gifting. Such a generous, public gesture," he laughed. "Hoping to endear yourself to the masses?" When his horse grew restless and tossed her head, Lyle yanked on the bit and tightened the reins. "I intend to put my name forward," he snarled as he took the paper from his tunic and held it out for them to see.

"As you should, if you feel so inclined – and entitled."

"Aye, asking for land that's rightfully mine. Seems more than absurd, but I'll take it piece by piece if I must. I'll have the lands and that woman hiding behind you. She's mine, aren't you Maggie? That was determined weeks ago, in this very glade. Right over there." Lyle gave his head a nod to the spot where he'd raped her. "This is hallowed ground, you might say."

"I think it's time you were on your way," Lennox growled. "Keep the notice and the date in mind. I look forward to seeing you in attendance." He walked toward

Lyle and slapped the mare's hindquarters, jolting her into action.

Chapter Twenty

"I want you to see it before the land-gifting event," Lennox said, kissing Maggie as they left The Weavers Hands. As they entered the glade, Maggie breathed a sigh of relief at finding it empty - two weeks had passed since Lyle had confronted them in the glade. She felt a twinge in her body but was able to look at the place where she was attacked with less discomfort and shame, thanks to Lennox and all he had come to mean to her. She felt him stiffen slightly, but he said nothing.

From a safe distance beyond the rustic chair, the doe and her fawn watched with alert, perked ears as they rode past. "Look at her fawn, Lennox - its spots are already starting to fade."

"You have to grow up quickly in the wild, I'm afraid. Human babies are fortunate - they have years with their parents."

"Yes, fortunate," Maggie whispered. She laid her head against Lennox's chest and closed her eyes. It was August, and her courses still hadn't come. She was nauseous in the mornings and always tired. The smell of cooking meat made her gag, no matter the time of day. She'd have to tell her father and Sorcha before she began to show. What about Lennox? She would have to tell him. She thought about the possibility of him being the father. The rape could have disrupted her courses, leaving her fertile the night she spent in the cottage with him. Sorcha said there were herbs that could end a pregnancy. Would she rid herself of Lyle's child, but not one fathered by Lennox? She didn't know who sired the baby she was carrying and chastised herself for giving herself to Lennox. If she hadn't, she could be certain. Now it was a question that might never be answered.

She would have to make a decision soon. The longer she waited, the greater danger she'd be in. She'd heard stories of potions that took the life of the mother as well.

"Are you alright, Maggie? You seem preoccupied. Is something on your mind?"

She roused herself and searched for a reason to give him. "I'm fine, but I realized that no one at your home knows about me, or has met me. There will be gossip. Are you prepared for that?"

"Don't worry yourself, mo chridhe," he laughed, squeezing her to him.

"What does that mean?"

"It's Gaelic for 'my heart.'" He took her hand, kissed it, and held it to his chest. "It would make me proud to hear that people think you're mine." They stopped at the stable that was still under construction. The roof was in place, but stalls were still being constructed along with a staircase leading to the hayloft above. The smell of fresh hay and new wood filled the air as Lennox helped her down and introduced her to Gavin. His rough, weathered hands took Titus' reins as he turned him toward the stable. He bowed slightly to Maggie. "Mistress."

Maggie gasped in awe at the huge manor house still under construction. The yellow-grey walls rose up at least two stories with long lancet windows in solitary spans or in groups of two or four. The top of the walls were crenellated, like those of any fine castle.

Stonemasons were carving the Brodie coat of arms into the surface on either side of the entrance below the date of 1277.

"Do you like it?" Lennox asked, taking her hand. "It will be called Brodie Manor."

"It's strong and beautiful at the same time. I love how it's open as it faces us and nestled close to the forest at the back. Welcoming and private."

"The land-gifting event will be held here on fifteenth day of August, the day after Market Day. I hope you'll attend." He took her by the arm. "Come. Let's have a look."

"When will this become your home?" Maggie asked as they crossed the threshold.

"Perhaps by Christmas. The exterior is nearly secure, but there is still a lot of work to be done inside."

"Tell me about the land-gifting event."

"I have more than I need, and there are people who can use it to provide for their families. It will be a memorable event with plenty of food and drink for those who attend."

"It's very generous of you and such an uncommon practice." She took his arm and smiled up at him, her heart warmed by his generosity.

Lennox described the location of the parcels of land as they entered the cavernous great hall. Massive oak beams supported the three- sided open gallery on the second floor with walls covered in wooden panels and stonework. Workmen were securing the large, oak mantle above the fireplace; they nodded and turned back to their task. The flagstone floors echoed their steps as they made their way to the wide, timbered staircase leading to the second floor. They talked about the window coverings, rugs, and tapestries ordered from Angus and where he thought they would go.

The last room they visited was in the east corner. "This room shall be mine," Lennox whispered, pulling Maggie to him. "I hope you will come and see it once it's finished."

"Yes, I shall, if you invite me," Maggie laughed, kissing his nose.

"Consider it done." Lennox took her by the hand and led her down the stairs. "I think it's time for some refreshment, agreed?"

"Aye, Sir Brodie," Maggie teased with an elegant, sweeping curtsy.

Darby met them at the door, greeted Lennox, and graciously responded to his introduction of Maggie. They went into the kitchen where Corliss welcomed them, giving Lennox a wink and knowing smile. "So, you've been to the big house, then," she said, serving them cool cider and gingerbread. "You're going to have to hire more help, Lennox. Goodness knows I can barely keep up as it is."

"Yes, I know. You keep reminding me."

"Well?"

"Okay, I give you my word. We'll work on it before the land-gifting event. Prepare a list of names, and you can speak to those you may be interested in hiring if they attend."

"I'll hold you to your word," she said, laughing and wagging a finger at him.

Lennox performed a mock bow from where he was sitting, and Maggie laughed under her breath at the warmth and ease of their relationship. Corliss turned to the stove as Lennox took Maggie's hand and gave it a swift kiss. The blush of her cheeks rose, and then faded, replaced by pale, white skin, damp with perspiration.

"It'll be roast venison for supper tonight – will you be joining us, Maggie?" Corliss asked, setting the roast in the pan on the stove and stoking the fire. It sizzled as it browned, sending the aroma of cooking meat floating through the room. Maggie's chair scraped the floor as she rose and ran out the back door. Lennox jumped up, but

Corliss motioned for him to stop. "I'll handle this; you best stay where you are."

Corliss closed the door behind her and pulled a cloth from her apron pocket. She crouched next to Maggie, holding her until she finished vomiting. Turning behind her, Corliss dampened the cloth in the water bucket next to the door and handed it to Maggie, along with a ladle for a small sip.

"Is it what I think, and not just a dislike of venison?"

"I'm afraid so."

"Does Lennox know?"

"I haven't told him yet, but it appears I'll have to now."

Corliss gathered Maggie up and helped her to a bench outside the door. "I'll have Lennox bring Titus 'round and see you home. You can tell him when and where you like. He won't hear it from me."

"Thank you, Corliss. You've been most kind."

"Think nothin' of it, lass." With a hug and a quick kiss on the cheek, Corliss disappeared inside. She returned to sit with Maggie, holding her damp and trembling hand.

Within minutes, Titus galloped around the corner with a concerned Lennox astride.

"She needs a gentle ride home, Lennox. Nothing over a walk, do ye hear?"

"Aye, I hear." He reached down to lift Maggie into the saddle and turned Titus around. They rode in silence past the huge manor house, across the clearing, and into the glade.

"Please, can we stop here a moment?"

"What is it, Maggie? Are you going to be ill again?"

"No, but there's something I must tell you, and I want to do it in private. This is as good a place as any." He helped her down and guided her to the rustic chair. He saw her settled, then knelt and looked into her eyes.

"I'm ready to hear what you have to say." He took her hands, kissed each one in turn, and held them in his.

Maggie took a deep breath and looked around; the glade was unusually quiet. Perhaps the heat of the day prompted the creatures that lived here to rest and doze until the cool of late afternoon. One small sparrow pecked at the leaf litter, then flew up to its nest as it chirped for its mate. She looked into Lennox's dark eyes, her own filling with tears. "There's no easy way to say this," she began.

"Then just tell me, Maggie. Out with it." Maggie's hair fell across her lowered face. "How bad can it be? You and I are here, together, and we love each other." He lifted her chin with his finger so that her eyes were forced to meet his. "Tell me, Maggie," he whispered, giving her hands a gentle squeeze.

Tears coursed down her cheeks and dotted the skirt of her gown. "I'm with child, Lennox."

He sat back on his heels, letting her hands slip from his. His eyes never left hers, searching their depths for an answer or an explanation that would never come. The silence was deafening and seemed to last forever.

She wiped her cheeks and stood over him. "Won't you say something, Lennox?" He remained kneeling and silent, head bowed as he listened to her heart wrenching sobs and retreating, running footsteps.

Chapter Twenty-One

Lennox felt removed from the world as if he inhabited someone else's body in another time and place. He didn't know how long he'd been there, hunched over and silent, but the forest was coming to life after its afternoon nap.

Titus was dozing next to a solitary pine and stirred when Lennox pulled himself up. With leaden feet, he walked over and hugged the stallion, took the reins, and trudged home.

"She told you then." Corliss stood, arms folded, after putting a steaming bowl of pottage on the table in front of him. Lennox nodded, staring at it, unable to take a single bite. "You have to do right by the young lass," she chastised. "Don't you see, Lennox?" She sat across from him and slapped her hands on the table, pulling him out of his fog. "What did you say when she told you?"

"Nothing."

"Nothing? What do ye mean, nothing?"

"Nothing. Not one damn word. I didn't know what to say, and then she was gone." He slammed his fists on the table, clattering everything on its surface. Anger seethed from his pores and brought color to his face. "Tell Darby to bring some wine brought to my room. Now, please."

"Is there no way to determine who fathered the child?" Angus asked, wringing his hands as he paced back and forth in the sitting room.

"I'm afraid not," Sorcha said. "The closeness of Maggie's intimacy with both Lyle and Lennox leaves the matter unresolved." She took Maggie's hands in hers. "And going on about this in front of her will not serve any purpose."

"Can we rid her of it?" He moved closer to Sorcha, asking in a whisper. "You must have potions and such – it could be done quietly and soon, aye?"

"That would have to be Maggie's decision. I can arrange it, but it will have to be done without delay. No courses since May, and it's August, so two months along, most like."

"What's to be done then, Maggie?" Her father stood impatiently like he did when a customer took too long to decide on a bolt of fabric. "I must get back to the shop."

The flutter in her womb validated what she felt deep down to be right and true. The baby might be Lyle's, or it might have been fathered by Lennox. She hated one man and loved the other, but there was no reason for an innocent to pay the price for the events in her life, tragic or otherwise. "I will have this baby, regardless of its parentage. It is a part of me, and I will raise it as my own, on my own."

"Heaven help us and the child," Angus sighed as he closed the door behind him.

The firelight danced through the burgundy liquid as Lennox twisted the corks but left them intact. His desk was cluttered with papers – lists for the various tasks that would have to be completed before his land-gifting day. Darby would delegate the completion of the posts for the banners, final preparations for the raised platform he would speak from, and the food and refreshments that would be served.

He worked late into the night, focusing on the plans to keep his mind from returning to the glade and the horrible outcome of it all. Maggie had confided in him, looked to him for love and support, and he'd met her vulnerability with silence. He tried not to think about how much he'd hurt her, knowing he'd have to find a way to earn her forgiveness.

He made a separate list for himself; its details would not be shared with anyone. That one he tucked into a valise with a few clothing items. The lists were left on the table with a note for Darby to oversee the final preparations. Lennox took advantage of the well-stocked pantry, saddled Titus, and left under the cover of darkness.

***

Maggie stood at the window, studying the delicate, pressed rose in the late afternoon sun. Lennox had given it to her the day he brought the picnic lunch to the glade. She loved him and thought he loved her. His affection made her feel warm, secure, and beautiful, but when she revealed her pregnancy something changed in him. His silence was uncharacteristic and letting her leave the forest alone was unchivalrous. Silent and absent. He hadn't been seen or heard by her since the afternoon in the glade nearly a week ago.

She felt herself growing thinner, having little desire to eat. The morning sickness and heartache took away what

little appetite she had. Working in the shop was a
distraction, yet something to endure because her father
needed her help. Maggie found it hard to concentrate. She
went through the motions of every transaction, smiling
politely while completing it as quickly as possible. With
every ring of the door's bell, a jolt of fear coursed through
her veins, thinking it might be Lyle coming to claim her as
his. One afternoon she saw him watching her through the
window. She escaped to the back room, cowering in fear
behind the bolts of fabric until her father came and ushered
her to her room.

Maggie breathed in the faint scent of the rose and
tucked it between the pages of her book. The shop was
closed and supper was not yet ready – a quiet, reflective
time when the distant hills shone gold before day slipped
into night. She wrapped herself in her cloak; Lennox's
scent clung to it, reminding her of their intimacy and all
that they'd shared at the cottage. It was a scent of the
outdoors, a bit of musky, wild animal, and strength. It lived
in the wool, triggering the tears that filled her eyes and
spilled down her cheeks. She sobbed quietly at the window,
willing him to appear, and then crumpled to the floor as her
knees gave way. "Oh, Lennox…how could you do this to

me," she whispered, her voice breaking. "How can you stay away when you said you loved me? Don't you know how much I need you, especially now?" Her chest ached with sorrow. Every beat of her heart was a painful throb as if it were truly breaking. He was out there, somewhere, but not here.

The sound of a galloping horse muted her sobs, unfolding her from the sorrowful heap where she'd collapsed. Maggie gasped and quickly wiped the tears from her eyes, thankful that Lennox had come at last. Joy turned to panic when she saw Lyle astride his horse, looking up at her window. She hunched down, crouched motionless, and covered her ears against his shouts until the hoof beats faded away. The tightness in her chest coupled with the uncontrolled trembling made her want to vomit, but she forced herself to breathe deeply, and the nausea gradually subsided.

Maggie pulled the cloak over herself and curled into a ball under the window, allowing time and exhaustion to blanket her like a heavy cloud. She dreamt of Lennox and the way he'd kissed her, held her in his arms, and made love to her. Her heart told her mind they'd be living in this

dream forever. There was no need to leave. She had
everything she'd ever wanted here with Lennox.

Who was tapping? It was distracting, irritating, and
it kept pulling her away from Lennox. The gentle,
persistent knocking finally roused her – an announcement
from her father that supper was served. "I'll be down
soon," she muttered. Her room was dark but for the light of
the rising moon, the streets quiet. She pulled herself up, lit
a candle, and washed the dried, salty tears from her face.
She'd had a dream, nothing more. Perhaps what she'd had
with Lennox was a dream as well – a waking dream, but a
dream nonetheless. All dreams end, good or bad.

Maggie stared through her reflection in the mirror
as she mechanically braided and tied her hair. She explored
the innermost recesses of her being, clinging to the parts
she'd need while casting off others. Love lived and
flourished in dreams, not in real life. Lennox became a
dream, one that faded away as they do – silent, without a
word. It had been warm, romantic, and sensual before it
transformed into a distant, painful memory.

She gazed at herself in the mirror and made a silent
vow. She would never love another man. Ever. She
wouldn't give her heart and soul to anyone the way she'd

given herself to Lennox. Her scarred and broken heart had suffered enough. She couldn't endure any more.

A movement in her womb brought her thoughts to the present and a protective hand to her mid-section. Perhaps she'd safely deliver a baby to love. It wouldn't be the same kind of love, but raising a child would bring some measure of peace and joy to her life. It might help fill the empty, torturous hours without Lennox, forcing her mind to think of other things. If she died in childbirth, so be it.

Maggie opened the door a changed woman – one who saw the only possible path forward. She accepted a life alone without Lennox, his love, and all that might have been.

***

Lennox collapsed on the grass along the bank of the stream and sobbed at the star-filled sky. He had tried to sleep in the cottage, but memories of Maggie and the intimate night they'd spent together closed in on him and forced him into the still, night air.

Years ago, he'd stared at the same star-filled sky as he positioned his men for a night raid - the night that fueled the terror-filled dream he couldn't escape. It jerked him awake, screaming and crying for forgiveness. The dream about the children.

It had happened in Spain, below the ramparts of Castle El Astra, in Teba. The Moors had led an attack on Lennox's troops, forcing them into a valley with no escape. Led by Lennox, they battled for three days, refusing to concede defeat even with the odds stacked against them. By the end of the fourth day, they had won the last battle and their freedom.

As night fell, he discovered a small cluster of twenty tents located south of where they had been fighting. Fueled by the need for revenge, he gave the order to attack. They began with axes and arrows, opening the flaps and killing anything that moved. Torches followed, setting every tent alight as a final measure and a beacon to any Moors lurking that Lennox the knight was undefeated and anyone in his path would pay with their life.

The screams of the dying and those being consumed by the flames brought whoops of joy and celebration to Lennox's troops. They hadn't lost a single man; victory had been swift and easy under Lennox's command. This would

be a battle to go down in history, to be remembered. A
battle led by the famous knight, Sir Lennox Brodie.

They waited until the first light of day to ensure
none remained alive before departing – a message loud and
clear to the Moors that had threatened to defeat them. The
camp was quiet as the men gathered at the far end,
preparing for the ride back to join the main group of
soldiers.

Lennox tightened his horse's girth and was lifting
his foot into the stirrup when he heard the moan from
inside a charred, smoldering tent. Instinct and reflex
propelled his actions as he slid his dirk from its sheath,
pulled back the flap, and stabbed the back of the barely-
moving body repeatedly until he was certain all life had
been extinguished.

As he turned to leave, he looked back at the body
one last time. It appeared smaller than a man. A dwarf,
perhaps? Hiding here because he'd have no chance in battle
against a full-grown man? There were others the same size,
all dead. Slowly and gingerly, he turned the body over and
came face-to-face with that of a young girl, perhaps six
years old. He stepped back in shock, his hand covering his

mouth in horror. What had he done? What had they all done?

"No, no, NO!" He screamed as he ran from tent to tent, tearing at the flaps only to discover the same, grisly remains. All of the dead were children, a hundred or more, none of them older than perhaps ten years. They were probably brought here to be hidden away from the main battle.

Alerted, the men ran over to where Lennox stood, ready to defend him against whatever enemy he'd come upon. He stood like a statue, his face frozen in shock, then fell to his knees and covered his head with his hands. "Children," he sobbed. "All children."

The crowd murmured and several looked inside the tents, returning with looks of horror and regret on their faces. Lennox's groom helped him into the saddle, took the reins, and led him away from the devastation they'd unknowingly created. The soldiers gathered together one last time before departing and swore a pledge of silence: never speak of what had happened.

Lennox did not speak for five days and slept only when exhaustion gave him no choice. Even then, he'd wake up screaming, the dead girl's face etched into his memory.

What little food he managed to eat he vomited minutes later. He lost weight, struggled to make decisions, and lost his temper with little provocation.

As the weeks and months passed, Lennox was gradually able to keep his meals down and return to functioning as a leader of his men. Sleep was elusive, and the dreams continued to haunt him. The shame and guilt he carried burdened him like a heavy stone in his chest. By the time he returned to Stonehaven, he had learned to mask his feelings and emotions with his silent, gruff manner. It was harder to escape the unpredictable triggers to his terror, like the cry or the touch of a small child.

Chapter Twenty-Two

The fully-risen moon cast a wedge of light from the window to the head of Maggie's bed. She settled under the quilt and studied its full, round face with disconnected fascination. In the quiet of night, she began to feel a gradual contentment with her decision and prayed that wherever Lennox was, he would find peace and happiness.

The world outside was uncharacteristically quiet as though it held its collective breath, knowing something was about to happen. The barking dogs were silent and the owls took wing into the forest to hunt mice. Even the air stilled as though given an order to hush by some unseen, divine authority.

Maggie drifted off, dreaming of gathering in the glade, filling her basket, and the scent of heather. Her dream moved to Lennox visiting the shop, but the scent of heather persisted and grew stronger. *This makes no sense,* her dream voice told her. *Something's wrong.* The sense of being watched forced Maggie to reluctantly abandon her dream. She woke to find a motionless, black figure silhouetted against the light of the moon, studying her.

It was as if her voice was strangled - the same feeling she'd had when Lyle had gripped her by the neck. She tried to scream, but all that escaped was a breathy whimper. How did he get into her room? She scrambled to the farthest corner of the bed and armed herself with the candlestick from her bedside table.

The figure took one step, and everything changed. The light of the moon captured his profile; the beard, aristocratic nose, and dark, wavy hair could only belong to one man. "Maggie," he whispered. "Oh, Maggie, my love."

He sat on the edge of the bed and gathered her to him. She allowed the tears to come, burying her face into the folds of his cloak, breathing in the scent of heather, and him. Instead of his rhythmic, secure breathing, she felt his chest jerk unsteadily. She looked up to see him biting into his large, rough fingers, fighting back the tears that would not be contained. He looked down and away from her, unable to meet her gaze as he tried to hide the pain and shame he felt.

"What is it, Lennox?"

"I'm destroyed, Maggie – can't ye see?" He stood with outstretched arms. "Gutted!" His entire body convulsed, overcome with sadness. He sunk to the floor and buried his face in the quilt to muffle his sobs and hide from Maggie seeing him weak and devastated. There was shame for him in that. He gripped her hand so tightly she could feel the bones grating, but said nothing. She slid to her knees beside him and laid her head on the bed next to his. Her free hand found its way to his thick, wavy locks. She gently took hold and cried with him, not knowing why, but moved to tears by his inconsolable misery. Never had she seen him so vulnerable, so broken, so utterly lost. She looked into his dark, grief-stricken eyes. "What is it?" she whispered. "What's devastated you so?" She gave his emotions the time they needed, holding and kissing his hands until he was able to speak.

His voice was halting and wavering, so unlike him. "I'm so sorry, Maggie."

"Yes, you were gone from me."

"I need to tell you why." He kissed the palms of her hands and held them to his chest. "It happened when I was away, fighting in the wars. I was wounded."

"But you're alright now. It's just a scar on your cheek..."

"No, Maggie, that's not it." He took her face in his hands, so she had no choice but to look into his. Lennox looked shy and embarrassed. "I was wounded somewhere else." He hesitated, clearly pained and reluctant. "We were fighting in North Africa and I was thrown from my horse. As I got to my feet, I felt a sharp pain between my legs. I thought my horse had kicked me as it struggled to its feet, but when I looked up, a Moor was standing over me with a bloodied sword. One of my archers killed him before he could strike a fatal blow." Maggie gasped and pulled Lennox to her. Lennox kissed her and continued.

"The next thing I remembered was lying on a table in a tent with a physician working over me. He said my ballocks were badly damaged. One was badly bruised and very swollen, the other sliced along one side. I was stitched, bandaged, and laid up for days. The physician said because of my injuries, I would never father children." With a heavy sigh, he looked at Maggie as fresh tears returned. "Don't you see, Maggie? The child can't be mine. Lyle fathered the baby you're carrying."

"And you don't want to be with me because of it?" Maggie tried to pull away, but Lennox tightened his hold. "I was raped, Lennox! Don't you…"

"Please, Maggie, please hear me out." He sat her on the bed and knelt on the floor in front of her. He cleared his throat and continued. "I've been carrying that knowledge with me for years and never paid it any mind. My wife was dead and buried, and I never searched for anyone to take her place. I was at peace with not fathering children until I met you." He took her hands and kissed each one in turn. "I went crazy with envy and rage when I learned you were pregnant because I knew the child couldn't possibly be mine. It's shattered me to the very core of my soul."

"Are you sure, Lennox? Are you sure it's not possible?"

He nodded silently. "The physician was certain. Don't you see, Maggie? I'll never be able to father a child with you, the woman I love most in the world. It's tearing me apart." He hung his head, looking defeated and hopeless. "I don't know how to come to terms with it. I'm a man who takes charge, who is in control of his actions and those around him. A man who gives orders and gets what he wants. A man who wins. But there's no winning here. I'm a loser, and I've lost to Lyle de Mortimer, the low-life scum who raped you."

Maggie took a deep breath as she turned to face Lennox. "So, where do we go from here? You can't bear the thought of me carrying a child that isn't yours? I will have this baby. It deserves to live and be loved, regardless of who fathered it."

She stood straight and tall and pulled Lennox to his feet. With one hand on each shoulder, she shook him and looked into his tear-filled eyes. "Lennox Brodie, I love you. Do I have your love in return?" Lennox nodded and managed a bit of a smile. "Then I want you to listen to me and listen well. As far as I'm concerned, you are the father of this baby, and no one, not even God, can change the way I feel. Being a father is more than planting a seed. It's loving, teaching, and nurturing the little one as he or she grows. There's no one on this world that can do that better than you. We can be a family if that's what you want. We have a chance for a happy life – you, me, and this baby. You have to walk forward with me and move past the things we cannot change."

Lennox drew Maggie into a strong, secure hug. "Aye," his broken whisper caressed her ear. "I can do that, and I will." He looked down at her, his lost, dark eyes searching hers. Then he turned away from her, shaking his head.

"What is it, Lennox? What's caused you to turn away?" She tugged on his sleeve and led him to the chair by the window. "Sit down and tell me. The air needs to be clear so that we can face the future together."

Lennox hung his head for what seemed like forever. Maggie pulled her chair closer to his and took his hands. "Take whatever time you need to gather your thoughts." Lennox nodded and stared at their clasped hands as he gently caressed hers with his fingers.

"There's something else. Something that happened when I was away fighting. I've never spoken of it and neither have my men. If you still love me after what I tell you, then all will be well between us."

"I know war is awful. Men do horrible things to each other, so I don't…"

"Please, I beg you. Let me speak before I lose my courage." In a soft, wavering voice, he looked into Maggie's eyes and told her about the night raid, the tents, and the children inside. When he finished, his chest heaved with emotional exhaustion. "Lennox Brodie is a knight, but not an honorable one. Are you certain you want to share your life with such a man?" He pulled his hands away. "I can see the answer on your face." He started to rise, but Maggie pulled him back.

"Will you do something for me?" Maggie stood and put her shawl around her shoulders.

"Of course. Anything."

"Then stay here, seated in this chair until I return. Your word?"

"I give you my word, Maggie."

She closed the door quietly behind her, listening to her father's snores as she descended the staircase and entered the quiet, darkened shop. She needed time alone to absorb what Lennox had told her. The Weavers Hands was her life – these bolts of fabric, dyes, and boxes of assorted decorative items her father imported when he ordered silks and velvets. Walking among the tables, she ran her hands over the soft, green velvet and the sturdy, woolen plaid. It was so familiar, so comfortable and secure. But that life was over. She would have a child in the spring, God willing. She looked out onto the darkened street to a spot where the light from her room cast a small, warm glow onto the rain-soaked ground. Her mind made up, she tightened her shawl around her shoulders and climbed the stairs.

Lennox stood as she entered the room with a tense, anxious look on his face. "Have you come to a decision, Maggie?"

"I have," she answered as she sat opposite him. "After tonight, we will leave what you told me in the past." Lennox nodded in agreement. "I hate war, and I hate killing. But that's what men do. It's what you swore an oath to do when you became a knight. But, the children..." Lennox shook his head, hung in shame. "Look at me, Lennox." She put her hands on his cheeks, forcing his eyes to meet hers. "You didn't know there were children in those tents when you attacked that night. You wouldn't have if you'd had that knowledge. Am I correct?" Lennox nodded but remained silent.

"Then you must forgive yourself and put it behind you. If we are going forward together, we have to leave the past behind." Eyebrows raised, Maggie nodded and smiled at Lennox, kissing his hands and holding them to her.

Lennox saw hope in Maggie's eyes, and he gave it in return – something he never thought possible. "So... you will have me then?"

"Yes, I will have you, Lennox."

"And do you really think I can be a good father to the child?"

"I haven't a doubt! I see it in you, Lennox. Just open your heart and let the babe in."

He pulled Maggie to him, kissed her deeply and tenderly, holding her close enough to feel the beating of her heart. He led her to the bed, pulled back the quilt, and motioned her under it. Lennox laid next to her, fully clothed and on top of the covers. He held Maggie in his arms with his cloak spread over both of them. "Aye, it's settled then."

The velvet night swathed the small room, giving rest and respite to the exhausted lovers who had fought for each other, their hope for a future together, and the unborn child. Mother Nature embraced them, alerted to their struggle and pain with each tear that touched the floor, and in turn, the world. The realm of the angels kept a silent vigil throughout the night – listening, helping, and healing.

When Maggie woke the next morning, Lennox was gone. In the spot where he'd laid his head was a pink, wild rose.

Chapter Twenty-Three

The fifteenth day of August dawned, clear-skied and full of promise. The banners lining the gravel drive flapped briskly in the wind; the Brodie coat of arms was both welcoming and menacing. They left no doubt in the visitors' minds whose lands they were entering. A banner with the same image spanned the platform where Lennox would announce the recipients of the twelve parcels of land he'd be gifting.

People began arriving late morning in family groups or broken, single streams. Dressed in their best, they chatted excitedly as they shared the information on the notices. A wild boar turned on a spit as Corliss supervised the placement of bread, fruit, cheese, and vegetables on the long, sturdy tables on either side of the platform. Chicken pies, pottage, and berry tarts filled them to nearly overflowing. A separate table held casks of beer, ale, and cider.

People moved among the tables, helping themselves to the generous spread before them. Musicians from Stonehaven arrived and took seats near the platform with their cithara, tympanum, and chorus. They began to play immediately, adding to the festive atmosphere.

The announcement would take place at half past two. Lennox watched the crowds approaching from his unfinished room in the manor house, and looked for Maggie and her father. She'd been unwilling to attend at first, knowing Lyle would be there to claim the Brodie lands and possibly her as well. Lennox convinced her to reconsider, assuring her that no harm would come to her. Angus was more than willing, seeing the event as a way to garner more business at The Weavers Hands.

A disruption in the relaxed procession caused Lennox to catch his breath and stiffen. It was Lyle, plowing through the crowd on his horse with a brightly-dressed entourage that looked like a flock of colorful birds compared to the muted colors worn by the farmers and herdsmen. His surcoat bore the azure and gold of the Mortimer coat of arms as did the caparison on his horse. "Welcome, Lyle," Lennox said to himself as he tightened the belt around his own with a jerk. "So glad you're here."

A movement to the left demanded his full attention and focus. It was Maggie, backing away from the group, hoping to go unnoticed. She pulled her father with her and stood hunched over behind a family of onlookers. Lennox turned heel, descended the stairs, and strode out to face the day.

He nodded in greeting to those he passed, but headed straight for Lyle, who dismounted and defiantly faced him. Lyle's cousin, Hector, stood shoulder-to-shoulder with Lyle until he elbowed him behind. Lyle wiped the corner of his mouth against the inside of his finger, licked it, and stroked his moustache in an attempt to straighten the wiry, untrimmed hairs. Lennox's greeting was a slight nod of acknowledgement and the barest hint of a bow.

"Ah, Lennox Brodie!" Lyle deliberately omitted the title of 'Sir' as he stood with outstretched arms, circling as he spoke to ensure he had the attention and ear of the onlookers. "The thief, the so-called 'hero' has returned victorious from the wars! It's a beautiful day for justice, is it not? We have plenty of witnesses gathered to see these lands finally returned to their rightful owner. Lands that are mine to rule as I see fit – with the iron fist of fairness."

"There will be no legal proceedings today. I am the law here. This day, and this land, is mine to give and take as I please."

"We shall see," Lyle laughed. "We shall see." They moved toward the platform, Hector following close on their heels. "Justice will be served to me as an apple in a roasted pig's mouth. The lands promised to me by my father and yours will pass into my hands today. They were stolen from me as a dog steals from a bitch when he humps her without permission." He dug into his nose with a grubby finger, twisted it around, and wiped the results on the front of his surcoat. He laughed at Lennox's reaction and brushed his hands against each other before spreading them out in front of him.

Lyle leaned his head toward Lennox. "Speaking of bitches – I see that you are alone today." He passed his fingers under his nose, and then waved them in front of Lennox, who backed away in disgust. "My fingers still carry the scent of a recently-explored whore. It's quite intoxicating, don't you agree?" A deep, sarcastic laugh erupted from Lyle's throat. "I'd have thought you'd grown accustomed to second-hand goods, Sir Brodie. Participating in the spoils of a hard-won battle has made you a connoisseur of cunts and the firm breasts of an unwilling, overpowered lass, has it not?"

Lennox stared ahead as he climbed the stairs to the platform. His body was tense and his eyes clouded with anger, but he refused to be baited by Lyle.

Hector stomped up the stairs behind them, grabbed Lennox's arm, and faced him, nose-to-nose. His brown, stringy hair trailed down his back, and his massive shoulders seemed to pull him onward as if he were leaning forward to take a step. His quick, darting eyes bored into Lennox's, then focused on the ground in front of him as he prepared to speak. He raised both arms into the air to quiet the crowd, his dirty, chipped nails fluttering like the banners. Nervous whispers and murmurs floated on the heavy, humid air, then hushed as Hector clapped for silence. "I need no introduction - you know who I am. Listen carefully!" he roared, pumping his fist against his open hand. "Or I'll knock your heads together." The music stopped and the sea of faces stilled but for a few whimpering babies. "Next to me stands a cowardly liar who traveled to fight holy wars, laid waste to children and old men, and fornicated with whores, mothers, and widows. How many bastards have his family's blood in their black veins? He is no knight." He laughed under his breath. "At least I swive those that are the same color as me."

The crowd shifted, looking at each other and muttering until Hector shouted for silence once again. He pointed at Lennox, who stood rigid as an arrow, eyes, blazing with rage, looking at the hundreds staring at him - looking at everyone and no one.

"This man, Sir Lennox Brodie, has no legal claim to these lands, yet he announces he will gift twelve parcels this very day. He is not a knight, nor a man. He is a drunkard, a coward who cares for no one but himself." Clapping wildly, he waved for the onlookers to join him. Some obliged halfheartedly until members of Lyle's entourage prodded and thumped their backs, forcing them to a more enthusiastic response.

Hector couldn't contain his ego and the thrill of being the center of attention. He ran his hands through his greasy hair and shifted his shoulders. "I challenge this coward to a one-on-one fight to the death, just like in the days of old. Winner takes all."

"No!" came a peppering of shouts from amongst the onlookers. Lennox kept his head solid and unmoving as a boulder, but his dark eyes scanned the uncertain, frightened faces. Every muscle in his body screamed for action, but he stretched his chest, clenched his fists at his sides, and let Hector continue.

"Hell, if Lyle here weren't the rightful owner, I'd be the master of all that ye see. The law says that defeat by death gives the victor the spoils." He turned and looked back at Lyle with a sneering laugh. "After Sir Brodie here, I could kill Lyle and become lord of that fine manor house. How 'bout that?"

Lyle's brightly-dressed companions frowned and shook their heads at Hector, warning him that he'd taken things too far. The natural world voiced its agreement as a jolt of lightning pierced the clouds, followed by a deafening clap of thunder. The crowd jumped in unison, the women covered their heads with their shawls as they pulled their frightened children close like hens protecting their frightened chicks.

"Sir Brodie, could we have the names, please? Before the storm hits?" Lennox recognized the farmer in the front row as Grant Stirling, one of the names on his land-gifting list. He welcomed the chance to breathe and loosen his chest. Raising a hand in agreement, he walked to the table and reached for the scroll. Lyle put his hand on it as if to be the one to read the names, but Lennox snatched it from his grasp with a snarl. "My lands. My gifting."

Chapter Twenty-Four

Lennox slowly turned to face the crowd, willing his face to relax enough to smile. A hush fell as they pressed together and moved closer to the platform, eager to hear the recipients' names in this unprecedented, land-gifting event. Lennox looked out over the swelling mass of humanity, nodded acknowledgement of friends and close acquaintances, and locked authoritative eyes with any would-be challengers. His gaze softened when it found Maggie – the fraction of a second enough to assure her a place in his thoughts, the swift hint of a nod acknowledging her significance and role in what was about to transpire. He cleared his throat and raised his hand for quiet.

"Thank you, one and all, for your presence today." His deep, gruff voice carried over the heads of those gathered, reaching the latecomers standing at the back. "I know of your hardships and challenges. The life you lead is not an easy one. I hope what transpires today will improve the lives of those who will be gifted. That being said, if the land brings you bounty, I hope that you will share with those who may be in need of your generosity."

The crowd murmured and nodded in response. The voluntary surrendering of wealth, this remarkable act of charity was unheard of in this place and time, and it would happen today under Lennox Brodie's authority. He unrolled the scroll and scanned the names he'd written. As he opened his mouth to speak, a sharp crack of thunder forced him to pause. He eyed the sky and waited until its deep rumbling finally died away.

"I will proceed as quickly as possible in hopes of your making it back to your homes safe and dry." Lennox felt Lyle just behind and to his side, precisely where he wanted him. Lennox had never liked Lyle, but had tolerated him in their early years. Since then, he'd become a puncture wound that refused to heal – irritating, infectious, and full of poison. Lennox was anxious to be rid of this wound which had intensified with Maggie's rape, but forced himself to focus on the task at hand. He began again.

"By the law of Scotland and as Sir Lennox Brodie of Clan Brodie, the rightful heir of these lands, I hereby announce the gifting of the twelve parcels by granting deeds to be signed by my hand and affixed with the mark of the Brodie seal." He paused as to scan the crowd but kept the whereabouts of Lyle and Hector certain from the corner of his eye. "By my authority, I announce the names of the twelve." The hundreds gathered before him clapped, cheered, then fell silent. "Alastair Cameron, Ross MacMillan, Duncan Fitzgerald…"

Lyle strode forward and pushed Hector aside. Hector responded by grabbing the front of Lyle's surcoat with a jerk toward the angry sky. The two struggled until Lennox punched his fist between them, jolting them into silence. "I'd like to finish, if you please." Lifting his arm, he finished reading the names and rolled up the scroll the rising wind was threatening to tear.

Lyle limped his way in front of Lennox and bellowed to the dispersing crowd. "I haven't had a chance to speak! I will be heard!" He scratched and grabbed at his crotch, rearranging his genitals as a way of advertising his masculinity. He cleared his throat, spewing a glob of phlegm over his right shoulder. Some returned; others made their way to the tables to take extra food home with them. The musicians tucked their instruments under their cloaks and slipped away. The sky darkened as the storm settled around them in an angry, suffocating embrace. "I am the rightful owner of the Brodie lands, and I demand justice here, now, on this day!"

Maggie stood next to her father, trying to become invisible now that Lyle had stepped up front and center to speak. She pulled her hood over her head and focused on the tattered boots of the farmer standing in front of her. She wanted to run but didn't dare move for fear of calling attention to herself. It wouldn't have mattered. Lyle's mismatched eyes and pointing finger targeted her. The farmer and those around her stepped back like the unfurling petals of a rose, leaving Maggie exposed once again.

Chapter Twenty-Five

Maggie's eyes pleaded with those of Lennox, begging him to help her. When he remained steadfast on the platform with his eyes upon her, she sagged with resignation and disillusionment. She gathered her cloak around her and looked past Lennox with an unfocused gaze.

"The Brodie banners fly before you, but these lands are mine, given to me on a deathbed promise to my father and the sire of Lennox Brodie himself." Lyle turned and pointed at Lennox. "This man is an imposter and a thief. He proclaims to be the lord of these lands, but he is false in more than just this."

Lennox looked into the eyes of friends and acquaintances who stared back in disbelief. He couldn't bring himself to look at Maggie, but a quick glance saw Angus move in and put his arm around her. He forced emotion from his face as Lyle continued.

"Lennox Brodie claims to have fought bravely in the wars in the name of God. That may be true, but what happened when the fighting was over? He fornicated with women as he chose, taking young lasses, mothers, and new widows without thought or consideration. He chose to satisfy his lust when and where the urge arose." Murmuring swept through the listening faces; some crossed themselves, others frowned and shook their heads in disbelief as they covered the ears of their children. Lyle turned toward Lennox, extending both arms towards him.

"So, this powerful knight returns from the wars, famous and wealthy beyond measure. But does he act like a lord, a man worthy of title and authority? Have you not heard or seen Brodie riding through his lands at all hours of the night, using God's name in vain as he screams into the blackest night sky? Have you not heard of his overindulgence of drink and that havoc that ensues? I ask you, are these the traits you would have in one who oversees your lands and all that transpires within?"

The remnants of the crowd shook their heads in disbelief and turned to leave, angering Lyle even more. Lennox refused to react but stared unseeing into the crowd, taking care to avoid the gaze of Maggie and her father. "Wait! I beg you! There's more you are going to want to hear!" Lyle turned to Lennox with a cruel, self-satisfying smile and rubbed his hands together in anticipation. "A lord such as myself needs a lady to stand by his side, to do his bidding and see to his every need." He puffed out his chest and with his hands called attention once again to his genitals.

"I intend to marry, and soon, for my intended is carrying my child." Unable to contain himself, Hector marched to the front of the platform and pointed his finger at Maggie. He continued pointing and giggling like a schoolboy until Lyle pulled him back and shoved him aside. "It wasn't much of a struggle, and it happened right here on Brodie lands, which are rightfully mine. So appropriate, don't ye think, Maggie?" Lyle kissed his fingers and extended them in her direction.

Lennox reminded himself it was going according to plan. His heart ached for Maggie's humiliation, but it couldn't be helped. He prayed she would understand and forgive his display of apparent indifference when all was said and done.

The people surrounding Maggie stared at her in disbelief. Some laughed, others moaned in sympathy. She wanted to run away and hide forever; she was beyond humiliation. She looked to the sky, praying for a lightning bolt to pierce the sky and take her life.

Hector stepped forward to speak, but Lyle grabbed him by the sleeve, spinning him around to face him. Lennox watched the two argue as he counted the seconds passing from the shaft of lightning until the inevitable roar of thunder. One, two, three...

As the thunder erupted, he pulled Hector's knife from its sheath and plunged it into Lyle's soft belly. Hector assumed the two men were in an embrace of agreement and reconciliation as he turned to the people watching the events unfolding on the platform. "You see? It ends well!"

Lennox knew the wound was fatal. The well-placed blade was routine for a fighting warrior. Something good and redeeming had finally come from his years of war and killing.

Lyle looked at Lennox as he clung to him, eyes bulging, unable to breathe a single word. He opened his mouth to speak, but gurgling, spattering blood took the place of any words that may have come. Lennox gave the blade a final twist as he lowered Lyle in front of him. As if in a cleansing response, the clouds opened, and the rain began to fall.

Chapter Twenty-Six

Lennox stepped away from Lyle's body as a raven
landed on his lifeless shoulder, cawing three times in a
proclamation of justice paid in full. A scream followed
from one of the onlookers, pointing at the growing trickle
of blood and Hector's embedded dagger.

"It's Hector's weapon!" a member of the entourage
announced. "He killed Lyle!" Lennox stood, arms
outstretched in empty-handed display, letting the crowd and
Lyle's companions determine Hector's fate. Hector looked
back in horror at Lennox, who stared back, shaking his
head with obscured, ambiguous meaning.

"Hector! Hector!" the people shouted over and over.
One man stepped forward, pointing at Hector. "He said
himself he'd be willing to kill Lyle to have the house and
lands. We heard it with our own ears!"

A member of Lyle's entourage stepped through the
people gathering closer to the platform. "He planned this all
along. He needs to pay with his life." The rest of Lyle's
men stepped forward onto the platform and surrounded
Hector. Screaming in protest, he kicked, hollered, and

fought at the ropes binding his hands behind his back. He became more animal than man in the midst of his rage and madness, and a wildness overcame him until he was subdued with a fist to the jaw. He was lifted onto a horse and led away with the hangman's noose already encircling his neck.

The storm raged on, its lightning casting a spotlight on Lyle's lifeless body, the rain diluting the seeping blood that had pooled on the platform. One of the men came forward, pulled Hector's dagger from Lyle's body, and heaved him over the back of an already skittish horse.

The violent lightning and thunder forced the unfortunate witnesses to flee. Soaked to the skin, they would be first-hand messengers willing to spread the word about the day's events and validate who was the rightful heir to the lands of Clan Brodie.

Lennox stood alone on the platform with outstretched arms and looked up at the sky. Rain streamed through his hair in rivulets, cascading down his cheekbones and chin. The heat of passion and anger was gone, leaving his skin chilled and his body shivering beneath his saturated clothes. Despite the cold, wet rain, he felt a sense of relief and peace as though his soul itself was being cleansed. His need for vengeance dissipated like the morning mist touched by the sun. Lyle's death had brought a sense of closure, ending the desire or need to take lives by violence. The ensuing guilt was something he was used to and expected. He'd taken the lives of others since he was a young man, and had grown accustomed to the quiet time that followed when he reflected on his actions. The lives he'd taken were a result of his sworn oath to his king. He was alive today because he knew he'd have to kill or be killed.

What he'd done today was different. A battle perhaps, but not a war. Or was it? He killed Lyle because of what he'd done to Maggie and what he would continue to do to her had he lived. He killed Lyle to save Maggie and the child she carried. Surely, God would not condemn him for an act of love, compassion, and protection.

He fell to his knees in prayer, head bowed in the rain, asking God's help to find Maggie. "Let her heart understand and forgive me for the pain and despair I forced her to endure. Let her know that everything I did, I did out of my love for her." As he whispered his thanks, the feeling of being watched drifted to him with the sheets of rain and demanded his attention.

Lennox stood, senses fueled with adrenaline as he braced for yet another confrontation. His hand grasped the hilt of his dagger as he peered through the driving rain at the solitary, motionless figure watching him from the empty, rain-soaked meadow.

His heart rejoiced at the sight of her. He stumbled down the rain-slicked steps in his haste to reach her, fighting the blinding wind and rain but feeling neither. Maggie ran to him, falling into the strong, enfolding arms that pulled her to his chest. He held her tighter than he'd ever done before, sobbing with relief as his warm tears mixed with the cold, pelting rain. Maggie clung to him, her body racked with pain and sorrow for all they had endured, separately and together.

It was over now. Maggie's public humiliation was at an end, and justice had prevailed. It was barbaric in its coming, but it had come. Lyle was dead, and Hector was swinging from the branch of a lone tree in some distant, desolate forest.

Maggie and Lennox huddled together as the storm raged on, oblivious to the elements, feeling safe and secure in each other's arms.

A tap on Lennox's shoulder brought them back to the reality of the world around them. Gavin handed Titus' reins to Lennox. "It's been made ready," he said softly.

"Please convey my thanks," Lennox said, patting his rain-soaked shoulder. "And to you, Gavin."

Lennox lifted Maggie into the saddle, settling her sodden cloak around her as best he could. He swung up behind her, guiding Titus through the softening rain, their solitary presence gradually fading until they were engulfed by the hushed, grey mist.

Also by Anne K. Hawkinson and Paul V. Hunter

THE SCOTLAND'S KNIGHT SERIES

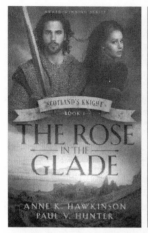

 annehawkinson.com  @annehawkinson

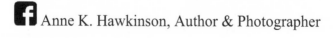 Anne K. Hawkinson, Author & Photographer

About the Authors

We connected across the ocean.

Anne K. Hawkinson

Anne was born in Duluth, Minnesota. The world's largest inland port became her "window to the world" when ships from around the globe crossed under the Aerial Bridge and docked in Lake Superior's harbor. Years later, she'd visit the countries that at one time existed only in her imagination. Anne lives in the United States.

Paul V. Hunter

Paul was born in Robroyston, Scotland. He is an award-winning short film maker, writer, and actor. He studies Scottish history and culture and participates in living history events. Paul brings the history of King Robert the Bruce to children through live storytelling, costumed as the king himself. Paul lives in Scotland.

Made in USA - Crawfordsville, IN
23553_9781732017504
04.04.2020 0515